MAIDA'S LITTLE SCHOOL

The Maida Books

By INEZ HAYNES IRWIN

→→→→→→→→←←←←←←←

Maida's Little Shop
Maida's Little House
Maida's Little School
Maida's Little Island
Maida's Little Camp
Maida's Little Village
Maida's Little Houseboat
Maida's Little Theater
Maida's Little Cabins
Maida's Little Zoo

Maida's Little School

BY INEZ HAYNES IRWIN

Grosset & Dunlap

PUBLISHERS

NEW YORK

COPYRIGHT, 1926, BY
THE VIKING PRESS

PRINTED IN U. S.

TO
INEZ ELIZABETH THOMPSON

CONTENTS

CHAPTER		PAGE
I.	An Evening in October	9
II.	What Kind of a School?	27
III.	M. La Flayosc Arrives	41
IV.	Mr. Lafayette Remains	53
V.	Miss White Arrives	62
VI.	Bunny Remains	71
VII.	Mr. Hood Arrives	84
VIII.	Robin Hood Remains	97
IX.	Halloween	105
X.	November	121
XI.	Christmas	131
XII.	Twelve Days of Christmas	144
XIII.	A Guess in January	155
XIV.	The Conspiracy	162
XV.	The Conspiracy Continued	166
XVI.	The Conspiracy Continued	172
XVII.	The Rift	182
XVIII.	The Girls Walk Out	190
XIX.	A Winter Picnic	198
XX.	Happy Days and Holidays	206
XXI.	The Preparations	213
XXII.	Mr. Westabrook Arrives	222
XXIII.	The Walk	228
XXIV.	Mr. Westabrook Digs	232
XXV.	Gifts for Everybody	240

MAIDA'S LITTLE SCHOOL

CHAPTER I

AN EVENING IN OCTOBER

DINNER was over in the Little House; and the Big Eight, as the eight older children now called themselves, had settled down to the evening's devices.

At one little table to the side, Maida Westabrook, Rosie Brine, Laura Lathrop and Dicky Dore were playing Mah Jongg.

A continued patter of pretty words made up the talk of this table. East Winds blew through the contest; West, North, and South Winds, though not so importantly. Green Dragons and White Dragons populated it. Flowers and Bamboo grew in it. High confining walls were built and broken, interrupted by an occasional crisp "Pong!" or "Quong!" and a final mysterious "Mah

Jongg!" It was quite as though instead of playing a game they were living in a fairy tale.

At a second little table, across the room from them, Harold Lathrop and Tyma Burle bent over a game of chess.

A continuous file of dignified personages marched through the talk of this table; "King," "Queen," "Rook," "Knight," "Bishop," "Pawn." Events of a martial nature occurred—castles were taken; royalties captured; church dignitaries, titled gentlemen, churls continually exchanged. Occasionally a stern "Check!" sounded and once a final jubilant "And mate!" It was quite as though instead of playing a game, they were fighting a battle.

Arthur Duncan—elbows on the table, head in his hands—pored over an enormous book at one end of the center table. Silva Burle, equally absorbed, read Louisa M. Alcott's *Eight Cousins* opposite him. Once, "Gee, Silva, this is a great book!" Arthur exclaimed. And, "You ought to read this one!" Silva declared.

Lounging in big comfortable chairs in front of the fireplace, Mr. Westabrook and Billy Potter conversed in low tones.

AN EVENING IN OCTOBER

Mr. Westabrook was doing the talking.

As he puffed at his pipe, Mr. Westabrook's powerful face bore a look of quiet serenity quite different from its normal air of scowling keenness.

Billy Potter was listening hard. The tangle of thick curls seemed to race off his brow in order to join a mop on top which made of his head a jungle of glittering gold. Under that thatch, his blue eyes alternately gleamed and glistened.

"School," the children could have heard them say, had they listened; and "teachers," "lessons," "supplies."

The door to the dining-room was open; and seated at the big table there, talking, were silver-haired Granny Flynn and black-haired Mrs. Dore, her daughter. Granny's long wooden needles emitted pleasant clicking noises, as a green sweater grew visibly under the urge of her swift fingers. With Mrs. Dore, needles, smaller and slower though of steel, seemed perpetually to race her mother's as they picked in and out of the Irish lace she was making.

"It was a foine day in April—" The children could have heard one of Granny's lovely stories had they listened; and Mrs.

Dore's emphatic comment: "She'll sup sorrrow with a long spoon of grief."

The background for this quiet picture was walls covered with rows of books, brightly-bound in scarlet, green, blue, and lettered in gold. Tall floor lamps, with parchment shades of deep gold, or pale-rose, bloomed like some new variety of air-flower, here, there—wherever there was a busy group. Great logs blazing in the fireplace sent tails and feathers and oak leaves of flame leaping up the chimney. Occasionally a pleasant hissing sound filled the rooms, as the fire found sacks of sap at the heart of the logs and turned them to steam.

The window-curtains were not drawn—they rarely were drawn, so remote and lonely was the situation of the Little House—and outside, so close that it seemed tangled in one of the great elms, a big full moon was silvering the autumnal scene of early October.

"Well, Billy," Mr. Westabrook concluded suddenly, "I think we'd better talk this over with them." He raised his voice a little, addressing the room. "I am sorry to interrupt your games, children, but this is very important, and as it concerns you more

AN EVENING IN OCTOBER 13

than anybody, I'd like to hear what you have to say about it."

"Oh, father," Maida Westabrook exclaimed, "just as Dicky and I were beating Rosie and Laura for the first time in a week." Her big gray eyes stared reproachfully at Mr. Westabrook from under their long dark lashes. Her forehead was damp from her efforts to win; her hair clung to it in moist, pale-gold tendrils.

"That's a tragedy, I'll admit," Mr. Westabrook commented. He turned his big bulk—with its heavy shoulders and powerful head it was no wonder that the papers always referred to him as "Buffalo" Westabrook—in his daughter's direction; smiling at her hectic look.

"We'll leave the game just as it is, Tyma," Harold Lathrop said to his partner. "Great thing about chess—isn't it—that you can pick it up any time."

The two boys rose together, taking the utmost pains not to disturb the chess-board. They made a strange physical contrast, Harold was stocky and strong looking—white-skinned, brown-haired. Tyma was as slender as a young sapling, but he looked as though he might have a sapling's toughness and elasticity. His hair was a dense cap of a smooth, purple-black metal; his skin, almost metallic too, a fine deep tan. Both boys showed a blue gaze; but whereas Harold's eyes were the thin azure of a summer sky, made paler by light lashes and brows, Tyma's were the deepest cerulean of a heavy sea, made bluer by thick black brows and lashes.

Different physically as were the two boys, mentally they were an even greater contrast. When Tyma—ragged, dirty, neglected—first joined the children in the Little House, Harold, who was always very fastidious about his appearance, held off from him. Suddenly they found they had an interest in common—games. Harold had always mastered games more easily than any other child in the Little House. He, it was, who taught Tyma croquet, tennis and chess. Harold was equally fascinated by the gypsy boy's main accomplishment—wood-craft.

Silva Burle, Tyma's sister, rose absently —it was apparent that her thoughts were still on her book—and helped the other children bring chairs and footstools to the fireplace. Even after she had seated her-

AN EVENING IN OCTOBER.

self beside Maida, an air of preoccupation hung about her. The two girls presented a marked contrast in type.

With her skin of an alabaster transparency, her eyes of a gray running-brook clearness, and her hair of a pale rippled gold, Maida was, strictly speaking, the most beautiful of the girls. Silva was, as certainly, the most interesting. She was slimmer than any of the other girls and as graceful as a reed blown by the breeze. Her flesh, creamy without color, but thick as a lily petal, showed a faint tinge of amber. Her hair, heavy without curl but fluid as molten metal, showed a deeper touch of amber. And her long eyes, luminous without sparkle, but velvety, as a pansy-heart, showed the deepest possible infusion of amber. Those eyes were a little plaintive in look; and in spite of her happiness at being taken out of the poverty and neglect of gypsy orphanage into the Little House, Silva's air was often sad. The three other girls—Maida, Rosie, Laura—were devoted to her; they showered her with all the little attention that their admiration could invent. Silva accepted them with a gentle gratitude; and yet there seemed to be some final barrier—of sensitiveness or sorrow—that their love could not break down. Only when Silva was with Nesta, her baby sister, was she utterly care-free and gay.

Arthur Duncan alone did not move. He was near enough to the group to join in their conversation; but his eyes kept stealing back to his big book; stealthily at intervals, he turned a page. A big, muscular lad, his black hair always shaggily tossed, his black eyes always intent, Arthur was not handsome like Harold or striking like Tyma. But having once noticed him, you continued to look at him. He had a quiet air of independence, of aloofness. And indeed, of all the children in the Little House, Arthur was most capable of taking care of himself; most self-sufficient; most inclined to live his own life.

"It's about your school," Mr. Westabrook began. "Now I——"

He was interrupted by a series of exaggerated groans from his auditors. "Oh we hoped you'd forgotten about the school, Mr. Westabrook," Rosie said. "We were so afraid that the new wing would turn out to be a school house."

AN EVENING IN OCTOBER 17

"No, I never had any idea of making anything but living quarters out of that," Mr. Westabrook replied. "But it's because I've been so busy with the new wing that I made no plans about the school. I had to get that done, you see, because you boys couldn't possibly sleep in the barn during the winter. Now there's plenty of room for you all in the house—and some guest chambers too."

"But we can go back to the barn in the summer, sir?" Harold asked anxiously.

Mr. Westabrook hesitated. Then, "You can sleep anywhere you want when the weather's warm," he declared.

"You boys are just like circus animals, you see," Billy Potter put in. "You have summer and winter quarters. But now," he added, "how about the school?"

Again the children groaned.

"Oh *Billy!*" Rosie exclaimed reproachfully.

And, "How *can* you remind him of the school," said Laura, "when you know we hate it so?"

"Mr. Westabrook might have forgotten it for another two months," Harold declared, "if you hadn't said that!"

Billy only grinned.

"But, I know just how you feel," Mr. Westabrook said sympathetically. "Still we've got to talk school at once. I shall be going to Europe in a few days; and I want this thing settled before I leave."

More groans.

"But, you must go to school sometime, children," Mr. Westabrook remonstrated. "All children go to school, and there's no reason why you should be exceptions."

"Abraham Lincoln didn't go to school, sir," Laura Lathrop interposed. Her big blue eyes showed a gleam of triumph as she cited this imposing fact. Laura had kept her summer's burn longer than any of them; and her slender figure had rounded. Her pink cheeks turned her blue eyes to blue flowers. Her hair, recently bobbed, had grown out in close little brown curls. She was prettier now than she had ever been.

"No," Mr. Westabrook agreed; "but he spent most of his young manhood trying to make up for it, studying and reading whenever he got the chance and often by the light of a pine-knot."

"But he probably studied the things he wanted to study, sir," Laura pointed out.

"Very likely," Mr. Westabrook replied, "and he also knew what things he wanted to study."

Laura laughed. "I don't want to study anything," she admitted.

"I'm afraid I can't depend on any one of you to turn out an Abraham Lincoln," Mr. Westabrook said. "You'll have to study like everybody else."

"Oh I hate school," Rosie Brine announced discontentedly.

"So do I," said Harold Lathrop.

"So do I," echoed Laura and Arthur.

"If we could only take ether the moment we entered the class-room," Rosie Brine suggested, "and didn't come out of the ether until school was over—so that we never remembered anything about it."

Just as Maida was the most beautiful of the girls and Silva the most interesting, Rosie was the most picturesque. Rosie's hair, eyes, brows and lashes were shining jet; cheeks and lips cardinal coral; her flesh, now that her tan had gone, gleaming snow. But it was not alone that Rosie was beautifully colored and shaped—she was full of life. And that life—a changing current—made the light in her eyes blaze, die down, flicker and blaze again; it illuminated the roses in her cheeks as though there were a perpetual flame behind them.

"Is what you learn in school any good to anybody?" Tyma Burle asked—not contemptuously, but as one genuinely curious.

"No," Arthur Duncan answered conclusively.

"See here," Maida broke in with spirit; "it's all right for you who have been to school all your life to talk like this. But I've never had anything but governesses. And I'm wild to go to school."

"I want to go to school too," Dicky Dore backed Maida up. "All the time I was lame, before Dr. Pierce fixed me up, I was too sick to go to school. Oh, how I used to envy all you!"

Some traces of Dicky's long illness remained on him. He was thinner than any of the rest, and there lingered in his face a faint look of strain. He was a brown-haired boy; with a skin formerly like wax; now a warm ivory. His eyes, of an Irish gray, were still faintly shadowed; his look

AN EVENING IN OCTOBER 21

was still a little too sensitive and quick.

"I'm one of those who want to study too," admitted Silva Burle. "All the time that Tyma and I were with the gypsies, there were two things I wanted more than anything in the world—to live in a regular house and to go to a regular school. I'm so ashamed of myself. A great big girl like me to know nothing about arithmetic.—And my writing is something terrible."

"I'll teach you arithmetic, Silva," Rosie offered swiftly. "I know I can do that because in school my teacher always put me to teaching those who were behind. But I can't do anything for your writing."

"Nor I," said Maida mournfully. "Father says my writing looks like hen's scratches."

"Well, I can," Laura announced with decision. "I always got a hundred per cent in writing. I'll help you."

"You'd better let Maida and me join the class too," Rosie said. "I'm always blotting everything. One of my teachers called me a sprinkling-cart."

"All right," Laura permitted, "you may."

"From now on, I'm going to call you teacher," Rosie threatened.

"All right," Laura agreed, "I'll call you sprinkling-cart."

The two girls grinned across the hearth at each other.

"I wish I had the chance to find out," Tyma declared thoughtfully, "whether I like school or not."

"Four of us are for school," Maida said, "and four against."

Mr. Westabrook addressed himself to Billy Potter. "I wonder why it is that children hate school? They always *do* hate it. I hated it myself. You hated it too, didn't you, Billy?"

Billy nodded.

Mr. Westabrook turned to the Big Eight. "Why is it that those of you who've been to school hate it so?"

Arthur Duncan answered him first. "I suppose the worst thing about it, sir, is that you're indoors when all the time you're crazy to be outdoors. You feel as though you were in prison."

"And, Mr. Westabrook, you have to sit in the same seat all day long," Rosie Brine added indignantly. "And it's a very uncomfortable seat. Then you can't speak to anybody. It's not natural for children to sit in the same seat all day long and not have a chance to talk with the other children about them."

"And I never had but two teachers yet," Laura Lathrop put in, "that I really liked."

"And I've never studied anything," Harold declared, "that I really enjoyed."

"There's something about the very idea of school," Rosie Brine explained, "that makes you feel so blue—especially at the end of a nice vacation. If you could go to school without knowing you were going to school—there might be some fun in it. But of course that would be impossible because the horrid old teachers would give it away.

"Yes, to go to school and not know it would be impossible," Mr. Westabrook declared. "It's a little like going to work and not knowing you were working. I'm afraid we can't conceal from you that you are going to school—eh Billy?" Under his heavy brows, he threw a quick questioning glance in Billy's direction.

Billy Potter did not answer. He seemed to be thinking of something else.

"But if we can't manage that you can go to school without knowing you are going to school, we can do the next best thing. And that's to have the pleasantest school that was ever invented. Now if you all have such definite ideas of what you *don't* like, you ought to have equally definite ideas of what you *do* like. And as I am going to have my way and compel you to go to school against your will, it seems only fair that I should, as far as possible, provide you with the kind of school you like. So I'll leave it to you to plan that. You talk the matter over among yourselves and decide on just what you want and I'll try to build it for you."

"Gee, that will be fun!" Arthur exclaimed.

"All right," Mr. Westabrook said rising. "I am pulling out early in the morning, so I'm going to bed now. Suppose you children have a conference tomorrow morning after breakfast. Billy will be here with you and he'll report your ideas."

"I know just what I want!" Arthur Duncan declared jubilantly.

"And I!" said Laura.

"And I!" said Rosie.

AN EVENING IN OCTOBER 25

"And I!" said Harold.

"And I haven't any idea what I want!" said Maida.

"Or I!" said Tyma.

"Or I!" said Dicky.

"Or I!" said Silva.

"Don't tell me now," Mr. Westabrook ordered, "what you want or don't want; I'm too tired to listen to you. Oh— one more thing, children. As you're going to be here all winter, I'm going to give you each an allowance of a dollar a week."

The Big Eight stared at Mr. Westabrook and at each other. Then they made a dash in Mr. Westabrook's direction. But he turned and ran up the stairs, a tail of children after him. He got to his room first and shut the door, locked it on them with a shouted good-night.

There was a chorus of reluctant goodnights and enthusiastic thank-yous as the balked children filed off in various directions to bed.

"What are you reading, Arthur?" Billy Potter asked as Arthur Duncan, returning to the living-room, slowly closed his big book.

"*The Life of Blanchemain the Pirate.* Gee, it's a great book."

"You're interested in pirates?" Billy asked.

"You bet!" Arthur answered.

CHAPTER II

WHAT KIND OF A SCHOOL?

THE next morning the Big Eight followed Billy Potter into the living room. Ever since breakfast, the children had been discussing something among themselves in low tones. Now they showed suppressed excitement; and as they came through the hall, the air was full of hissed whispers and exploding giggles.

"Now let's all sit about the big center table," Billy Potter suggested, "and you can give me your ideas about the school and I'll write them down. Let's go round the table in order. You come first, Rosie."

Rosie was all ready for the question. Her great eyes blazed with mischief. Smiles tried to break through her lips, but she held them back.

"Well, my idea of a school," she answered immediately, "is that it should be out-of-doors."

"Oh, but Rosie," Laura interrupted, "we couldn't study out-of-doors when it was raining or snowing."

"I've thought of that!" declared Rosie. "And you're right, you couldn't. But a lot of studies could be carried on just as well under the trees as anywhere else—reading and singing and—and—almost anything that you don't have to write. Of course I will admit that papers blow and rattle when there's a wind, but we could weigh them down with stones. We could hang maps and black-boards on the trees and we could build lockers for books against the tree trunks. That's when the weather's good. But when it rains, classes could be held in great glassed-in balconies, like sleeping porches, only bigger; so that you'd feel you were out-of-doors, even if you weren't. I'd like schools to be built in the midst of a great park, and some of the classes to be held in a garden and some in an orchard."

Rosie's ideas were greeted with applause from the rest of the Big Eight.

"All right," Billy said twinkling, but starting in an efficient way to make notes in his little red note-book. "Very interesting, I'm sure. Now you, Laura!"

WHAT KIND OF A SCHOOL? 29

"Well, the thing I should most enjoy in a school," declared Laura, quite as ready as Rosie, "would be to be allowed to get up and walk round and talk whenever I wanted to. I don't see why everything has to be done sitting down. And I don't see, when you do sit down, why you shouldn't have a comfortable chair and a comfortable desk. I should want a nice, big flat-topped desk for every child and one of those chairs you can whirl round in."

Again came prolonged applause from the audience.

"Swivel chair," Billy informed her as, still twinkling, he made more notes in his little book.

"Oh and I think every child ought to have a typewriter," Laura concluded.

"Your turn, Harold," Billy said, continuing to twinkle, but still writing busily.

"I'd like to have a school with plenty of supplies," Harold started off in the most fluent manner and in his most business-like voice. "I think there ought to be outside in the corridor, one closet entirely filled with nice clean blank books and another with nice clean paper, and a shelf-full of blotters. I think there ought to be one whole barrel filled with pen-holders and beside it a keg filled with pens. And then I think there ought to be another barrel—no a *hogshead* —filled with pencils—all with rubbers on the end. Everybody ought to have his own pencil-sharpener screwed on his desk, and a big, fat waste basket under it."

Harold's ideas proved more popular than any yet. The big fat waste basket was greeted with delighted smiles.

Billy Potter was now biting his lips hard to keep in his amusement. But he continued to take down these revolutionary ideas.

"What I want most," Arthur Duncan declared, without waiting to be told, "is a map room. I saw a map room in a public library once. Gee, it was a peach. I love maps. I even like to draw them. I'm for a big room with maps on every wall—maps of all the continents and all the big important countries and perhaps ten of the most important cities in the world—London, Paris, Berlin, Vienna, Rome, New York, and—and—well, I'm not sure of the rest. And in the middle of the room the biggest globe that could be found. So that when you were reading a book and wanted

WHAT KIND OF A SCHOOL? 31

to know where a place was, you could find it right away."

No applause greeted Arthur's statement. The Big Eight seemed too interested to move. They knew that Arthur was not joking, that he returned again and again to maps in some of the old books in the library. Hanging on the wall of his room was a small map of the county in which the Little House was situated. That had tumbled out of one of the broken-backed old histories in the library, and Mr. Westabrook had given it to him.

Billy's smiles too had disappeared. After Arthur ceased to speak, he seemed to fall into a brown study, pencil absently tapping his little red book.

"Your turn, Dicky," Billy roused himself after a while.

"Oh, I haven't anything to add," Dicky said. "I'm willing to go to any kind of a school."

"Me too," said Silva, "I mean I, too."

"I, too," echoed Maida and Tyma.

"Surely you have some ideas, Maida," Billy asked.

"I have some ideas," Maida said dimpling, "although I had to work hard to think them up. I was afraid they weren't important enough. But as long as our school is going to be in a great park——"

It was not Maida's phrase, "as long as our school is going to be in a great park," which produced the violent applause, but the assurance in her tone.

"—I suggest" Maida went on, trying to keep her lips from smiling, "that we have a zoo with lions and tigers in it and giraffes and zebras and bears and leopards. There could be great deep trenches dug to separate the animals who would eat each other up."

She was interrupted by shouts of assent from the other children.

"They could be kept in a little park of their own," Maida went steadily on, "surrounded by a big wall. There could be towers on the wall and we could watch the animals through the windows in those towers. Then we ought to have a great, big, enormous flying-cage for birds; and an aquarium."

"Why couldn't we have a great pool," Arthur Duncan added, his black eyes lighting electrically, "with hippopotamuses and crocodiles and alligators in it?"

Everybody groaned.

WHAT KIND OF A SCHOOL? 33

"And a snake jungle," Harold contributed, "with a great big boa constrictor—the longest in the world—in it."

Everybody shuddered.

"And a monkey-house," suggested Rosie, "with every kind of monkey in it."

Everybody laughed.

"And a stable full of elephants," Rosie added, "one for each of us, so that any time we wanted to take a ride on their backs, we could."

Everybody applauded.

"Then I don't see why we couldn't have a stable full of horses too, one for each of us!" Harold suggested.

"And a garage full of cars, one for each of us!" Tyma took it up.

"And an aerodrome full of flying machines, one for each of us," Arthur carried the idea out.

"This is certainly running into money," Billy commented. "I don't think it would cost less than a million dollars. Anything more?"

"Yes," Harold answered for the rest, "I think we ought to have a moving picture outfit. Then instead of having to study geography in stupid books, we could study it in the movies. It would be just like traveling through all the countries of the world. Talk doesn't teach you anything. But you know a good deal about mountains after you've seen hundreds of pictures of them."

"Well, whatever we decide," Billy went on, serious once more, "there's a lot of work to be done—architects to be seen; plans to be drawn up. But in the meantime we will be sending down supplies. Now I've got to get to work." He arose, putting his fountain pen and the little red note-book in his pocket. "It will be a long time," he remarked, "before the school will be finished. So that if you really don't want to go to school, you are very lucky children."

The children thought so too; for they waited only for him to get out of the room before they exploded in capers of joy.

"*Of course* it will take a long time to build a school!" Rosie said. "It took over a month to build the new wing with a double shift of men working all the time."

"And however long they think it will take, it always takes longer," Arthur declared. "I know enough about building for that."

"Why—why—why!" Maida stuttered, "I

WHAT KIND OF A SCHOOL?

can't see how school can possibly be finished before the spring. They can't work during the winter."

"That means," Laura exclaimed jubilantly, "that we probably won't have to go to school until next fall."

"Hooray!" said Arthur, "nothing to do all winter but enjoy ourselves."

"Hooray!" said Harold. "We can play all day long."

"And coast," said Rosie, "Hooray!"

"And skate!" said Laura, "Hooray!"

"And go off on sleigh rides," said Arthur, "Hooray!"

"And build huge snow houses!" said Rosie, "Hooray!"

Even the four of the Big Eight who wanted to go to school, joined in this hooray.

"Let's celebrate every holiday," suggested Rosie. "Let's see what holidays come next. First of all is Halloween."

A clamor arose. "Thanksgiving!" "Christmas!" "Valentine's Day!" "Washington's Birthday!" "Lincoln's Birthday!" "April Fool's Day!"

There was more jubilation. The Big Eight clasped hands and danced round the table. All except Arthur Duncan, who sat down at the huge book which lay just where he had left it the night before. Suddenly a sharp "Listen!" from him brought them to silence.

"Say," Arthur went on, his eyes full of a black shining, "listen to this. This book is all about Blanchemain the Pirate. It says that on his way back from his pirate expeditions in the Spanish Main, he used to stop at an island, just off the coast of Massachusetts. There has always been a legend that he buried some of his treasure there. What do you think the name of that island is?"

The others only stared.

"Spectacles Island!" Arthur informed them.

"*Spectacles Island!*" Tyma repeated.

"*Pirates* on Spectacles Island!" Harold exclaimed.

"*Treasure* on Spectacles Island!" Dicky Dore gasped.

"The book also says," Arthur went on, "that Blanchemain landed often on the coast near Spectacles Island. Do you realize that's here—near where we live?"

WHAT KIND OF A SCHOOL? 37

"Let's start digging for treasure at once!" Laura suggested wildly.

"Let's swim over to Spectacles Island!" Maida suggested even more wildly.

"Let's go up into the Tree House and look at the island!" Rosie suggested practically.

With one accord they tore out of doors. The Little House was connected with its barn by a line of glassed-in rooms. Through the roof of one of these grew a great oak; and built into the tree, about ten feet above the roof, was a little house. Two flights of stairs, one to the roof and one up the tree, led to this house. The children dashed breathlessly helter-skelter over the stairways. Once inside the Tree House, they crowded about the window facing east. They stared, for a moment silent as though they were gazing on some magic sight.

Across the distance stretched the heaving plane of the Atlantic Ocean, gleaming green and silver in the crisp October air. A pair of islands, rocky but thickly wooded, broke, sharply black, out of the sunny glare and lifted high above the water. A narrow strip of rock connected them.

"Have you ever been on Spectacles Island, Maida?" Rosie asked at last.

"Only once," Maida answered.

"Don't you remember anything about it?" Arthur asked.

"Almost nothing." Maida tried to answer this question patiently, although she had answered it many times before. "I remember only that there were trees—lots of trees, very big and high, and beautiful grassy places—and a little pond."

"Oh!" Dicky exclaimed, "it sounds like a fairy tale. Can't we get over there someway?"

"I'll ask my father to let us sail there next summer," Maida declared.

"Just imagine the pirates," Arthur said in an awed tone, "coming sailing up from the south and anchoring between us and the island. "I don't *think* they could get right close up to the shore—they'd have to land in small boats. And then they'd bring the treasure onto the island. Great chests full of pieces of eight and——"

"What's pieces of eight?" Tyma asked.

"Gold money," Arthur answered. "And Spanish doubloons and——"

WHAT KIND OF A SCHOOL? 39

"What's Spanish doubloons?" Tyma asked.

"Gold money," Arthur answered. "And great ingots," he went on.

"What's ingots?" Tyma asked.

"Bars of gold," Arthur answered. "And watches and swords and jewels——"

"Diamonds and rubies and emeralds and pearls," Rosie broke in. "Just think, there may be great boxes of them buried on the island. Why it must be just like Sindbad the Sailor in the valley of jewels over there."

"And beautiful necklaces," Laura said dreamily. "And rings and bracelets and maybe crowns. Oh how I'd like to find a crown." Her voice died away in a murmur.

"They'd be fearful-looking men—Blanchemain's pirates," Arthur went on, "with fierce black eyes, and long black hair and great scars on their faces. Blanchemain had only one eye. He always wore a black patch."

Again, for a fascinated interval the children stared at the heaving level of water.

"Oh, isn't it too bad," Maida said in a

heartbroken voice, "that we can't ever see what's happened long ago."

"If only somebody would invent a magic telescope!" Silva sighed. "And when you looked into it you could see anything that's ever been."

CHAPTER III

M. LA FLAYOSC ARRIVES

DURING the next few days great bundles were constantly arriving at the Little House from Boston and New York. They filled the hall and one end of the living room. The children guessed that these were supplies for the school, but as they had no authority to do so, they made no attempt to open them. The Big Eight did not find time hanging heavy on their hands, however.

It was true that they missed the little children, who had been sent to their own homes for the winter; the Doyles—Timmie and Molly; the Clark twins—Dorothy and Mabel; and most of all mischievous Betsy Hale. But Delia Dore, Dicky's sister, and Nesta, Silva and Tyma's sister, tried their baby best to fill these vacancies. Tiny black-eyed Nesta was still too young to do anything but sleep and eat and sleep again.

Little copper-headed Delia, in the talkative and mischievous period between three and four, was the pet of the household, however.

Left so much to their own devices, the children split into groups. After doing the chores, the boys ranged the woods. The girls stayed at home, for they still helped in the household work; engaged in odd jobs of sewing and cooking.

"I wish the boys would ask us to go on their tramps with them," Rosie said discontentedly every time they started.

And "So do I," Maida always echoed.

Arthur often worked in his room on the maps which eternally engaged his attention. Silva toiled over the problems in arithmetic which Rosie set for her every morning, and the writing for which Laura gave her a copper-plate copy every afternoon. Although each night found them a re-united group, reading or playing games or talking together in front of the big fireplace, during the day, they met as a group mainly at mealtimes.

"Oh, it isn't as nice as in the summer," Rosie said sorrowfully one day to Maida.

M. LA FLAYOSC ARRIVES 43

"Then we big children did everything together."

"Well, Rosie," Maida pointed out to her, "You hated the thought of school and that was something we *could* do together."

For a week, the Little House seemed strangely quiet; then suddenly excitement exploded again.

Billy Potter telephoned to Mrs. Dore that he was coming to the Little House for the week-end and that he was bringing a guest with him—a Frenchman. Billy gave Mrs. Dore the name of his friend and spelled it for her—La Flayosc; but the pronunciation was a little too complicated for her to remember. After he had finished talking with Mrs. Dore, he called Maida to the telephone. Maida could remember the name easily enough, although she could not afterwards repeat to the Big Eight all the things Billy told her. But she did remember Billy's final admonition. "Tell the children that he doesn't speak a word of English and they must be as considerate of him as they possibly can."

There was always a sense of thrill in the air when Billy Potter came to visit the Little House. His favorite week-end train arrived Friday morning; and after breakfast that day, none of the children stirred out of the house. They sat in the living room, talking disjointedly, their eyes constantly wandering to the window.

Suddenly, "Here he comes!" Tyma exclaimed. Tyma's gypsy-trained ears always heard sounds long before the others. "Here comes the bus!" It was a point of honor among the Big Eight to refer to the fine big automobile which Mr. Westabrook had put at the disposal of the Little House as the "bus."

The children filled the doorway as Zeke drove the car up the driveway. And when Billy Potter alighted, they threw themselves with such violence on him that for a moment, they did not notice his companion. It was Billy indeed who said, "Come, come! You must meet Monsieur La Flayosc."

Monsieur La Flayosc was a little round short man; middle-aged and showing it in the silver flecks which flashed from his grizzled hair and the silver sparks which struck from his pointed beard. But somehow the instant he spoke, he seemed young too; for his eyes lighted with a youthful brilliance when he smiled; his long flexible eyebrows

M. LA FLAYOSC ARRIVES 45

lifted at the corners with a youthful energy when he laughed. There were patches of a deep winey color on the olive skin. He was mobile in expression; quick in movement; pliant in gesture.

A little shyly the children shook the hand the stranger extended to them; listened with as understanding a look as they could muster to the flood of French he poured upon them. Maida alone—for Maida not only had lived much abroad, but had had French lessons from the moment she could talk—answered him with a flow of language almost as swift as his own.

When he entered the living room, Monsieur La Flayosc emitted a startled exclamation. He stood in the center of the room, pivoting and expressing his admiration in a series of sharply-snapped and exquisitely articulated adjectives.

"I know what he's saying!" Rosie Brine declared suddenly. "He likes this room. He's saying it's magnificent."

Monsieur La Flayosc's eyes sparkled. "Magnifique!" he said again, "Magnifique!" The others caught the inflection of admiration though the meaning was quite obscure. Monsieur La Flayosc repeated a long string of adjectives very slowly. **Then** "Grande!" he ended.

"Grand!" Laura suddenly translated, "I know *grand*. Oui! Oui!"

Everybody laughed. But only Maida knew that the French *grande* was not the English *grand*, but the English *big*.

"Have the supplies for the school come yet?" Billy Potter asked.

"There are loads of boxes and bundles here," Arthur answered. "Oh, how crazy we've all been to open them!"

"Well, let's open them now!"

For the next two hours the wildest excitement reigned in the Little House. First of all—Billy had mercy on Arthur—came maps. Maps and more maps and even more maps. Mr. Westabrook had given orders, Billy told them, to place these maps temporarily in the front room leading off the hall, opposite the library. When the school was finished, they could be transferred to a new big map room which was to be built there. Putting them up required carpenter's skill; and Zeke, who possessed accomplishments of this kind, was called in to help.

All day long the three men, assisted by the Big Eight, worked at this job.

M. LA FLAYOSC ARRIVES 47

When dark came, the short wall beside the door held maps which rolled up, like curtains one over the other, of the five continents. Opposite, hung the hugest map of the United States which the children had ever seen. Across the long wall stretched in groups of five, maps of the twenty greatest cities in the world. These also rolled up curtain fashion. From the fourth wall protruded—"just like a drier for dish towels," Rosie described it—a sheaf of maps of various countries. On a low table in the center of the room stood a huge, beautifully colored globe. The children inspected the maps with varying degrees of interest, but they could not seem to tear themselves away from the globe.

There appeared also among the parcels a roll of maps very old and very faded, stained; sometimes cracked and torn; and— because they were made before people knew the whole extent of the world—very inaccurate. These, Mr. Westabrook's instructions read, were for Arthur's own room. Almost, these old maps interested Arthur more than the new maps. Strange mediæval ships were sailing on their unbounded oceans; horrific sea monsters lifted their heads above their rearing waves. Countries were strangely shaped; cities and rivers curiously spelled.

The children had never seen Arthur so excited. For an interval he would lose himself, studying these antique parchments. Then, as though hypnotized by some sudden thought, he would rush to the map room and lose himself, either in contemplation of one of the fresh new wall maps, or the great globe. Then, as though he were answering another inward call, he would rush back to the old maps again. By night these latter were all thumbtacked onto the walls of his big room in the new ell.

In the meantime, the rest of the Big Eight were occupying themselves with the other bundles; blank books; paper; ink; penholders in various colors, so that every one of the Big Eight could always identify his own; pencils (with rubbers on the end), pens, blotters, erasers.

Monsieur La Flayosc was indefatigable. He helped hang the maps; he helped carry the supplies to the upstairs closets where, it was decided, they should be stored. He talked to the children whenever he passed them; and although they did not know one of the words he used, they sometimes got the idea of his phrases—especially when he asked questions.

"En haut?" he would say, both expressive hands pointing upwards; and somehow they knew he was asking, "Upstairs?" Or *"La bas?"* he would demand, pointing downwards; and in just the same way they would know he was asking, "Downstairs?"

He was so gay about his own inability to understand, so explosively clear in the pronunciation of these strange questions and directions, so full of the most swift and illuminating gestures, that after a while the Big Eight got the sense of a whole sentence, even when they still could not have said what a single one of the words meant. In the middle of their talk at the table that night, he suddenly broke in with a question.

"He says—" Maida began to translate.

"Don't you tell us, Maida," Rosie ordered. "Let's try to find out for ourselves what he's saying. I always feel that I'm *just going* to understand him."

It was as though Monsieur La Flayosc understood her. He lifted his glass. "Le verre!" he said with a comic little uplifted twist to his eyebrows. The children all lifted their glasses. "Le verre!" they chorused. Swiftly Monsieur La Flayosc, his eyes twinkling brown fire over the warm patches of winey color on his cheeks, lifted his plate, his knife, his fork, his spoon, his napkin—each time giving the French name. And always the children repeated it after him. It got to be a delightful game. Before the meal was finished—and it finished in an uproarious mood—they were asking each other in French for the salt, or the sugar, or the bread. They had even learned to say, "S'il vous plait!" (If you please!) And "Merci!" (Thank you!)

After dinner they sat about the fire talking. Occasionally Monsieur La Flayosc would ask a question. It was always a very short question. But although often he had to repeat it again and again, because his expressions and gestures told so much, always in the end they managed to get what he was asking without Maida's help.

"I think he's a perfect *darling*," Rosie exclaimed as she went to bed. "Oh I do hope he will come to visit us often."

"He makes me think of a great big robin red-breast," Laura remarked.

M. LA FLAYOSC ARRIVES 51

"He makes *me* think of a pouter pigeon," Harold said.

"Gee, and he knows all about maps!" Arthur put in. "I heard him telling Billy the greatest amount of stuff—just pouring it out. I knew it was about the maps because he kept pointing to them. Oh, gee, how I wished I could understand him! I'm going to keep talking to him until I do understand him."

"Monsieur La Flayosc is awfully hard to say," Rosie said. "Oh I know what to call him, I know. Let's ask Billy to ask him if we can call him Mr. Lafayette."

"I won't ask him," Billy said, "but I'll tell you how to ask him. Now stand up in line there."

The Big Eight stood in line. Billy stood in front of them whispering. Monsieur La Flayosc regarded them with quirking eyebrows and an indulgent smile.

"Now!" Billy said.

In unison—a little floundering as to pronunciation—the children called, *"Peut-on vous appeler Mr. Lafayette, Monsieur La Flayosc?"*

Monsieur La Flayosc's eyes filled with

their characteristic brown fire. "Oui, mes enfants!" he consented heartily. "Oui! Oui! Oui!"

His *oui's* were like tiny word explosions.

Sunday night, as the time approached for Billy and Mr. Lafayette to leave, the children's spirits sank a little.

"Oh, Billy," Rosie said, "do bring Mr. La Flayosc here with you again."

"Bring him here again!" Billy repeated, "Why, didn't I tell you he isn't leaving? He's going to stay and visit you for a while."

"Stay with us!" Maida exclaimed "Isn't that wonderful!"

The others gathered about Billy with, "Is it really true?" And, "How long will he be here?"

"Just as long as you make him happy, I fancy," Billy answered. "He has some writing and studying he wants to do, and your father told him that he'd find this a good place to do it in. But you must try to talk with him as much as possible."

"We will," the children chorused.

"And don't let him get lonely," Billy entreated.

"We won't," the children chorused.

CHAPTER IV

MR. LAFAYETTE REMAINS

NEVER had a stranger come to the Little House whom the Big Eight liked so much as Mr. Lafayette. They liked him so much indeed that when he was with the Big Eight, life became one prolonged struggle to communicate with him. He was with the Big Eight a good deal; walked when they walked; played when they played; sat with them during the quiet evenings when they read or engaged in games. The effort to understand him and to talk to him seemed for a while to grow no less difficult.

It continued to be the greatest possible fun, however.

Their meals were punctuated by continual bursts of laughter as they struggled with strange pronunciations. Mr. Lafayette was always so patient, always so willing to explain, always so interested in what they were doing, always so delighted to listen to and join in talk that they vied with one another as to who should take the first faltering steps in making him understand. Of them all, Tyma made the swiftest progress—that is all except baby Delia. At the end of a week Delia was already cooing words in French.

The days were really very gay. And then one morning further enchantment broke. A minute after the bell rang for breakfast, the sound of music coming from the piano in the music room, flooded the house with a magnificent vibrancy.

"It's the Marseillaise," Maida called to Rosie. "It must be Mr. Lafayette."

"Isn't that the French National Hymn?" Laura asked. "I can't pronounce the French name."

"Yes," Maida answered. "Say the name after me—so that you can surprise Mr. Lafayette with the French pronunciation."

Laura and Rosie and Silva murmured "Marseillaise!" "Marseillaise!" "Marseillaise!" until they had caught Maida's accent.

Suddenly, accompanying the marching accents of the music, Mr. Lafayette began to sing. "Oh, what a beautiful voice!" Rosie said.

"Baritone," Laura informed them with a touch of superiority.

The voice seemed to fill the house with French patriotism. The girls tore through their bathing and dressing to get downstairs. One behind the other, the boys came marching to the gallant music into the living room.

Mr. Lafayette smiled and nodded, but he went on playing. Maida, who knew the French words, joined in with him. And before they went into breakfast they all sang the chorus of the noble hymn in French— as they caught fragments of it from Mr. Lafayette and from Maida—mixed inextricably with English.

That night after dinner, Mr. Lafayette again sat down at the piano and began very softly to play and sing. Gradually the children left their games and books and gathered about him.

"Oh, I know what this is," Maida exclaimed at once, *"Sur le Pont d'Avignon. On the Bridge at Avignon.* Oh please teach it to us, Mr. Lafayette. It's such fun."

Mr. Lafayette immediately jumped up

from the piano. Ranging the boys in one row and the girls opposite them in another, he drilled them in one of the oldest and most beloved of the French nursery rhymes;

Sur le pont d'Avignon,	On the bridge of Avignon,
L'on y danse; l'on y danse;	Everybody dances; everybody dances;
Sur le pont d'Avignon,	On the bridge of Avignon,
L'on y danse tout en ronde.	Everybody dances, round and round.
Les petites filles font comme ça;	The little girls do like this (the girls bow);
Les petits garçons font comme ça.	The little boys do like this (the boys bow).

Mr. Lafayette had great difficulty in teaching the boys to bow in the elegant manner the song demands—from the waist, one hand over the heart. At first they were self-conscious, blushing and grinning foolishly; all except Harold, who always excelled in whatever demanded quickness and grace. But Mr. Lafayette's entire lack of diffidence soon gave them the necessary social courage.

The girls of course performed their answering curtseys—one foot stretched far back, the hands lifting imaginary hooped skirts and the body gradually sinking very low—with the greatest enjoyment.

Sometimes Mr. Lafayette would greet the girls in the dining room mornings with one of these low bows. The girls of course instantly sank almost to the floor. Sometimes meeting a boy in the hall, a giggling girl would drop an elaborate curtsey. The grinning boy of course dipped low in answer. Gradually the boys learned from Mr. Lafayette to pull the chairs out from the table for the girls and to seat them.

The Big Eight got into the habit of singing for an interval every night. They learned two more songs equally famous and equally beloved by the French people: *Au Clair de la Lune* and *Malbrouck.*

Au Clair de la Lune tells the story of Pierrot and Columbine. This is the first verse—Columbine singing it outside Pierrot's door:

Au clair de la lune,	In the light of the moon,
Mon ami, Pierrot,	My friend Pierrot,
Prête-moi ta plume	Lend me your pen

Pour écrire un mot.	To write a word.
Ma chandelle est morte;	My candle has gone out;
Je n'ai pas du feu;	I have no fire;
Ouvre-moi ta porte	Open your door
Pour l'amour de Dieu!	For the love of Heaven!

Mr. Lafayette made that song lilt and leap like a bird.

Malbrouck, the tune of which some of them had heard their parents sing—the old song, *I Won't go Home Until Morning*—tells the story of the great feudal lord Malbrouck. In the first stanza he marches gaily and triumphantly off to war—marches off to the sound of jubilant tramping feet, the caroling trumpet and drum; his lady-wife waving to him from the castle walls. In the last stanza, his body comes back from the war—comes back to the sound of sullen marching feet, the muted trumpet and drum; his lady-wife weeping on the castle wall.

The chorus to *Malbrouck* is a single three-syllable word, "Mironton, mironton, mirontaine"; or "Mironton ton! ton! mirontaine!" Mr. Lafayette sang the first

MR. LAFAYETTE REMAINS 59

verse; those *mirontons* sounded like tiny silver bells chiming. But when at the end the dead Malbrouck came back, those same *mirontons* boomed like great brazen bells tolling.

Presently there appeared on the piano a a series of short, very wide books which contained a great many French nursery rhymes set to music. They were most exquisitely illustrated by a French artist who, the Big Eight soon gathered, Mr. Lafayette admired very much—Boutet de Monvel. They got into the way of singing these songs together. It was not surprising—because it was so simple—that the children learned the music very soon. But it was astonishing—even with Mr. Lafayette's clear enunciation and the fact that Maida caught them so quickly—how soon they learned the words.

"Let's plan a surprise for Mr. Westabrook when he comes home," Harold said one evening. "Let's learn a lot of these French songs so that we can sing them to him without looking once at the book."

That idea pleased everybody. But they really did not need any such inciting motive; it was fun enough just to sing the lovely airs—shouting the gayer choruses at the tops of their voices. One of them alone—Silva—was more interested in the pictures in these song-books than in the songs themselves. She spent long intervals studying them; the soft pastel colors seemed to fascinate her.

But Mr. Lafayette's accomplishments weren't all singing. Sometimes in the evening, he would seat himself at the piano and without singing, just play. Always if he were about, Dicky, who passionately enjoyed music, took a place at his side; his eyes gleaming, his face getting paler and paler as an inner excitement increased. Always too, Harold followed Dicky; took up a position on the other side, watching Mr. Lafayette's accomplished fingers with a concentration second only to Dicky's. One by one, the others would be drawn from their games to the piano, as though the big ebony box were a monster magnet—until only Arthur was left, poring over his old maps and his *Life of Blanchemain the Pirate.*

Those intervals of playing were the beginning of something new in the Little House. How it came about nobody could afterwards exactly remember. But presently, they were all learning to play the piano—all except Arthur, who never even tried. Indeed the interest of most of the others waxed and waned eccentrically as the winter went on. But Dicky and Harold never lost their interest; never failed to practice faithfully.

CHAPTER V

MISS WHITE ARRIVES

IN the middle of the next week came another telephone message from Billy Potter. Again, after talking with Mrs. Dore, he called Maida to the telephone.

"Maida," he explained, "I'm bringing another visitor to you this week, Miss White—Marion White. She's the author of the Little Tourist books— You remember those books that some of you children were so interested in."

"Oh, yes, I've read them all," Maida answered. "Oh, I'm so glad she's coming. Is she as nice as her books?"

"Nicer!" Billy said with emphasis. "Now I want you all to give her as cordial a welcome as you possibly can."

"Oh, we'll do that," Maida promised.

"All right then—good-bye!" Billy finished the conversation.

Maida skipped back to the Big Eight with her exciting news.

MISS WHITE ARRIVES

"Oh isn't that interesting!" Laura exclaimed. "Miss White will be the first author I've ever met in my life. I love the *Little Tourist* books."

"I don't believe I've read them," Dicky said.

"I certainly haven't," Tyma asserted.

"And I never even heard of them," Silva declared mournfully.

"What shelf are they on?" Harold asked.

"On the left-hand side of the library," Rosie answered instantly, "near the window. They're all bound in the same dark blue."

Dicky skipped into the library and came back with his arm full of books. He distributed them about.

"Don't give me one!" Rosie said, "I know them by heart."

"And so do I," said Laura.

Already Arthur had seized *Little Tourists in Italy;* was turning over the leaves.

"This looks very interesting," he said, "and very nice pictures. It's about Rome. Sometimes I think I'd rather go to Rome than any other city of the world. There are so many ruins there." His tone was absent and even while he spoke, his eye caught half-way down a page, and continued to engage itself there. His voice ran down to silence.

"Perhaps she will be writing one of her books while she's here," Maida said. "Won't it be interesting to watch a book being written. Perhaps we'll learn how it's done."

"Oh, how I'd like to write a book!" Silva exclaimed.

"I guess everybody would," Laura said.

"Well, I am going to take this book on Rome," Arthur came out of his absorption, "that is," he added with the new politeness that had come to them all with Mr. Lafayette's arrival, "if nobody else wants it."

"I'd like to read one, too," Dicky said.

They divided the Little Tourist volumes haphazard among their group.

"It will be so much easier to talk with her," Maida approved, "if we have all read one of her books."

"What do you suppose she'll be like?" Rosie asked.

"I know exactly how she'll look," Laura answered in a convinced tone. "She'll be—she'll seem—she'll—" Laura's flounderings came to a full stop. She giggled.

MISS WHITE ARRIVES

"What made me say I knew exactly what she'd look like, when I haven't the least idea in the world?"

"I always feel," Maida said, "that I know exactly how people are going to look. I seem to see them. And then when I meet them they never—never—*never*—are the least bit like what I expected. One funny thing is," she went on wrinkling her brow in perplexity, "that you'd expect I'd be so disappointed, that I wouldn't like them. Almost always I *do* like them though. But the funniest thing of all is that after a while, I can't remember what I thought they were going to look like. It all passes out of my mind."

"I think she'll have gray hair parted in the middle, and she'll be kind of stout," Rosie said.

"So do I," Laura agreed.

"She will look sort of like a teacher," Rosie went on, "a *nice* teacher I mean. Like a teacher, but a little like a mother too."

"She'll wear glasses!" Silva prophesied.

"That's exactly the way I feel about it," Maida agreed.

The boys listened to these remarks; but

obviously their thoughts wandered. Apparently Miss White's appearance interested them little. And from that time on, although they read or looked over her books, they displayed no curiosity about the author.

The girls talked of her continuously however. Their last words at night were of the expected guest; their first words in the morning. The day of Miss White's arrival, they themselves dusted her room, gathered a vase full of the last asters in the garden; put on the reading-table the magazines which Billy Potter had brought on his most recent trip; arranged beside it a pretty thermos-set. As the day went by, their anticipation increased in curiosity rather than diminished. They chattered about it with Mr. Lafayette; in their excitement producing an atrocious mixture of French and English. Mr. Lafayette, patient as usual, substituted his French phrases for their English ones; made them repeat them after him. But there was an air of waiting even about Mr. Lafayette.

"Do you know," Rosie said once, "I think he's just as excited as we are."

Exactly on the moment, Zeke drew up in

MISS WHITE ARRIVES

front of the door—drew up with a flourish. The Big Eight, crowding into the doorway, greeted Billy Potter, as he leaped out of the automobile, with their usual welcoming shouts. But Billy waited only to wave to them. He reached into the machine, produced one after another, two big black suitcases, a typewriter; then held out his hand to——

A tiny hand reached from inside the car and took his hand. A head appeared in the car door. A slender figure hopped out of the car.

Rosie clutched Maida and Maida clutched Rosie. Silva emitted a soft breathed "Oh!" Laura dropped an astounded giggle. The boys stood and stared.

Was it a child that had emerged from the car?

No, not a child but a girl—but a young girl scarcely bigger than a child. Not exactly that, but at least she was scarcely taller than Laura, who was the tallest girl in the Little House. Curls of a soft brown appeared under the edges of her little hat. Eyes of a soft brown turned the gayest—the friendliest—look on the group of children. And at the surprised stare with which the Big Eight greeted her, that friendly look broke into a wide grin. Dimples, pressing into pretty hollows the soft rose of her cheeks, appeared when this smile appeared; disappeared when it disappeared. But the lovely cleft in her chin stayed there permanently.

In another moment she was shaking hands with them all.

"This is Rosie!" she was saying with the utmost certainty. "And this is Arthur. And Dicky and Maida and Silva." She went through the group, identifying them all, without waiting for an introduction. "Oh yes, and Laura and Tyma and Harold. I feel as if I'd known you all my life."

The children watched amazed at this magic power.

"How did you know us without ever having seen us?" Maida gasped.

"A little bird," Miss White answered smiling, "told me about you."

But Rosie all the time stared at Miss White. "We thought," she said in an awed tone, "we thought you were going to have white hair parted in the middle. And wear glasses—and look like a school teacher."

MISS WHITE ARRIVES

Miss White laughed.

"You don't look as if you were old enough to write books," Silva commented in an astounded voice.

Miss White laughed again.

"You look just like one of us," Maida declared.

Miss White laughed once more.

"If a lady so young can write books, why can't anybody learn how?" Laura said.

Miss White laughed for the fourth time. "Anybody can," she admitted.

"Then why can't we?" Rosie asked.

"You can!" Miss White informed her.

In another moment, they were all taking her to her room. It was apparent at once that she was one of those young women whom boys like. Without being told, the boys of the Little House possessed themselves of the suitcase; golf bag, tennis rackets, package of books, umbrella. The girls fussed about, helping her to take off her long outer coat, placing it on a hanger in the closet, putting her little hat on the shelf; and with her permission starting to draw water for a bath.

All the time she herself was unpacking the suitcase, placing toilet articles on the dresser, photographs on the desk-top—giving them the drollest accounts of her trip to the Little House; how in the first place, she had nearly lost the train, because she stopped to watch some boys spinning tops; how she nearly rode past the station because of a gypsy sitting opposite who insisted on telling her fortune. The gypsy had prophesied that she was going to make a lot of new friends.

"You see she told the truth," Miss White stopped to say cheerfully.

CHAPTER VI

BUNNY REMAINS

AFTER a while, the Big Eight left their guest alone; went down stairs, obviously one intention animating the group: to hang about until Miss White joined them. She entered the living room presently as though she were dressed for a party, in a little white gown and slippers with sparkling buckles which made her look more than ever like a child. Billy and Mr. Lafayette appeared immediately and Billy introduced his companion to Miss White. For several minutes Miss White talked with him in fluent French. Never before had the children strained so hard to understand. It soon became apparent that, whenever she talked to Mr. Lafayette, she was going to speak French.

"We've got to brace up and get to talking soon," Harold said to them in a whisper, "or we're going to miss an awful lot."

Indeed they were missing something already. Mr. Lafayette was so amused at what Miss White said that his brilliant eyes closed up tight, his mouth opened wide on his roar of laughter.

Dinner was an uproarious meal, for Miss White suggested that every one in turn should say something to Mr. Lafayette in French. And somehow the struggles of the children—although Miss White helped them—and especially the struggles of Billy Potter—for Miss White refused to help him—had never seemed so comic before.

In the living room after dinner, Dicky first put the question that was trembling on all lips.

"Miss White," he said, "will you tell us how people write books? You see, you're the first author we children have ever met. And we've talked about it a lot and we all want to know."

"It's the easiest thing in the world to write a book," Miss White answered, smiling mischievously. "All you do is get an idea for a story and then sit down and go to work."

That sounded so magically easy that for an instant no one of the Big Eight said anything. And then, practical as usual,

"How do you get the idea for the story?" Rosie asked.

Miss White laughed—a laugh so full of rippling silver that though they had not the remotest idea what they were laughing at, the children joined her.

"Oh, that's a dreadful question for you to ask, Rosie," she said finally. "Because getting the idea is the hardest thing about it. However, you just have to think and think until the idea comes to you."

"By jiminy, I'd like to write a book," Arthur declared.

"Oh, so would I," Silva breathed.

"I should think when you were writing a story," Maida said, "that you'd feel as though you were living in that story."

"That's exactly the way you *do* feel," Miss White agreed.

"Oh, it must be fun!" Arthur commented.

"Well," Miss White exclaimed electrically, "would you children like to write a book?" She looked enquiringly around the circle. "You can, you know, if you only think you can."

Eight pairs of eyes stared at her in a moment of paralysis; then the Big Eight were all on their feet capering about the room.

"Well then, why don't you start?" she asked. "Writing it together, of course. I'll help you. I'll show you exactly how it's done."

The little group burst into a clamor of questions.

"One at a time," Miss White laughed. "Let's be quiet and talk it over."

For an hour they talked it over. On the initial idea and that alone they were unanimous—that they wanted to write a book. But on what the subject of that book should be, there were as many ideas as there were children. A boy wrecked on a desert island was Arthur's idea; a quartette of boys hunting in the West, Tyma's; Dicky suggested a hero who became a great musician. Rosie suggested a heroine who was a tomboy. Harold proposed for a hero a boy who would grow up to be a great golf or tennis or chess champion. And Silva proposed for a heroine a little girl who lived all alone in her own house and took care of it. Maida said that she didn't care what the book was about, so long as there were fairies in it. Laura said that *she* did not care what the book was about, so long as there were *no* fairies in it.

For a moment they seemed to have struck a deadlock. Then Rosie made one of her acute observations. "We all want to write stories about what we like most or what we'd like to have happen to us."

The last words had scarcely left her lips when Silva said in her soft voice, "It would be wonderful to write a book about the wonderful things that have happened to us."

"About us!" Maida said, her eyes getting big with wonder.

"As we are *now!*" Rosie added, her voice growing deep with excitement.

"Gee, that would be great fun," Arthur approved.

"*The Adventures of the Big Eight,*" Harold threw off in an electric voice.

There was a pause while everybody considered this title and then everybody burst into exclamations of approval.

Miss White during all this had said nothing, only—very attentively—listened. "That seems to please you all," she commented. "*The Adventures of the Big Eight.* It is a very good idea for a first book because, you see, each chapter could be a separate adventure, and you could have as many chapters as you wanted—six, eight, ten, twelve."

"I don't suppose our chapters could be as long as those in the *Little Tourist* books?" Harold said.

"No," Miss White agreed. "They may not be a half, or a third, or perhaps even a quarter as long. A chapter may be as long or as short as you want to make it."

"Let's start tomorrow!" Dicky suggested.

"Let's!" "Let's!" "Let's!" came from over the group.

"We will start whenever you want," Miss White said. "I am just exactly as excited about it as though it were my own book. You see, I'm writing a book myself; another *Little Tourist* book—*The Little Tourists in the Southwest*. Suppose we race each other to see who'll finish first. Of course I'm older and a more experienced writer. On the other hand, there are eight of you. You read me your chapters as fast as they're finished, and I'll read you mine."

Maida voiced the feeling of the Big Eight. "That will be wonderful!" she said in a solemn tone.

"But how are we going to do it?" Rosie asked.

"Well, since I have had so much more experience writing books than you," Miss White replied, "I hope you won't be offended if I make a suggestion. The thing to do first is to select your adventures; then choose one for the first chapter, and talk that over. Each one of you should write that chapter. When you have finished it—and we must set a certain date at which it must be finished—we will read every one of them aloud. Then you can vote on the one you like the best. The author should copy his adventure carefully—on the typewriter, I think—and that will be Chapter One of your book."

"Then all we have got to do now," Rosie said, "is to choose the first adventure that we want to write about."

"Exactly," agreed Miss White.

A prolonged discussion followed. At first nobody could think of any adventure that the Big Eight had had. And then Maida suddenly said, "Remember the little boys who bothered me so when I opened the Little Shop? And how Arthur stopped them?"

"The Adventure of the Bad Little Boys," Miss White suggested.

"And how Dr. Pierce fixed up Dicky's leg," Arthur said.

"The Adventure of the Cured Leg," Miss White suggested.

"Oh, and when Betsy found the baby deer," Rosie burst in. *"The Adventure of Betsy and the Baby Deer,"* she named it herself.

"The time Tyma and Silva frightened us at the picnic," Harold swung in, *"The Adventure of the Picnic."*

"And—oh, what a dumb-bell I am—the time I found Nesta in the cave," Maida contributed again, *The Adventure of the Cave— the Cave—the Cave-Baby."*

They went on and on; and Miss White let them go on. Finally she told them that she thought it was time to choose the first adventure. After another discussion, the Big Eight decided that they would take the adventures in the order in which they happened, and that the first chapter should be called, *The Opening of the Little Shop.* And then they talked over that important day.

Their memories were many and varied.

First of all Rosie spoke. "I never shall forget when I first saw Maida, how I envied her hair. Of course, having black hair, I always wanted golden hair. And I loved Maida's hair because it wasn't in curls like mine, but sort of wavy and—and—rippled—all over her head. How Maida could have that hair bobbed, I don't know," she ended severely.

"I hated Maida," Arthur Duncan declared simply.

All the rest of the Big Eight stared at him aghast and then burst into laughter. Arthur laughed himself. "I thought she was one of those good little girls that I'd always despised. Of course," he turned in explanation to Miss White, "I was a pretty bad boy myself. That's why I hated good little girls."

"Believe me," Rosie interrupted, "you had nothing on me. I was a terror."

"You certainly were," Arthur agreed. "Why, Miss White, Rosie and I used to hook jack about twice a week."

Miss White stared at him questioningly. "Play truant, I mean," Arthur explained. Oh, it was the longest time before I grew to like Maida. Sometime, maybe, I'll tell you what she did that made me like her."

Arthur's eyes went very far away. Maida blushed furiously.

"But of course," Laura took up the story, "all the children in the neighborhood were terribly excited about the Little Shop. An old lady had kept it for years." Laura was now addressing Miss White. "Her name was Mrs. Murdock. We used to buy a lot of things there, but it was a very untidy, dusty sort of a shop. And when we saw that it was all being painted over and papered, and that the rooms upstairs were being fixed up for somebody to live in—oh, we could hardly wait to see what it was going to be like."

"The great thing," Dicky broke in excitedly, "was when the sign went up over the door—MAIDA'S LITTLE SHOP."

"Oh, it was a beautiful sign," Maida sighed. "The letters were gold but the sign itself was a lovely blue. How proud I was of it!"

"What I noticed particularly," Harold contributed, "was the toys that you first put in the windows, Maida. There were a lot of things that girls like—dolls and little furniture. But what interested me were the things boys like—games and marbles, and there was a top of a kind I had never seen. I saved up for days and days to get one."

"Oh, what a good time we had that winter!" Maida commented, a far-away look in her eyes. "I'd love to live it all over again."

"I wouldn't," Rosie declared stoutly. "This is going to be the most beautiful winter I've ever known."

"Well, you see, Rosie," Maida explained, "my lame leg got well, and I could play just like other children."

"But think how you'll play this winter," Rosie persisted. "You wait!"

It was quite apparent from the talk which followed that the children agreed with Rosie. Nevertheless, their enthusiasm continued as they went on describing to Miss White the first days of the Little Shop.

Last of all they agreed that every one of them, even Silva and Tyma, who had not been a part of the group when the Little Shop was opened, should make an attempt to write this first chapter tomorrow.

"And now," Miss White said, "let's have a spelling match!"

The evening ended on a note of the wildest

hilarity; for the first spelling match lasted a very short time. Everybody failed on *Mississippi* except Billy. But in the second spelling match, even he failed on a word pronounced *tissic* and spelled *phthisic*.

"And the worst of it is!" he remarked ruefully, "I failed on it once before when I was in school!"

The children of the Little House had never before realized what bad spellers they were.

When the children accompanied Miss White to her room, they found it—everything unpacked—in what Laura described as "spindy-spandy" order.

On her desk, framed in carved silver or scarlet leather, were a group of photographs. Some were signed and above the signature of all was written, "To Bunny."

Rosie read these two words in a questioning voice.

"Yes," Miss White smiled, "that's my nickname. Everyone who knows me well enough calls me Bunny."

"Oh, Miss White, can we—" Rosie began, and stopped, flushing furiously.

"Can you call me Bunny?" Miss White

asked for her. "I was just about to suggest it. I'm not comfortable with any other name."

And Bunny she instantly became.

CHAPTER VII

MR. HOOD ARRIVES

AT the end of the next week, Billy Potter called Maida to the telephone again. "You will think after this, Maida," he said, "that every week I am going to bring down a new guest. But this is the last—a Mr. Robert Hood—a very delightful man. I think you will like him just as much as Bunny or Mr. Lafayette."

"Billy," Maida said earnestly, "that hardly seems possible. "How could there be three such nice people in the world?"

"You wait, Miss Skepticism," Billy said.

"What does skepticism mean?" Maida, who loved new words, instantly demanded.

"You look it up in the dictionary."

"Tell me how to spell it."

"S-k-e-p-t-i-c-i-s-m!"

Maida went back to the dining room. "Billy's bringing down—s-k-e-p—another guest at the end of the week—t-i—his name is Mr. Robert Hood—c-i-s-m!"

MR. HOOD ARRIVES 85

"Maida, have you gone crazy?" Rosie demanded.

"No—I'm just trying—skep—to remember a long word, Billy—ticism—called me—skep— Wait, I'll look it up in the dictionary—ticism."

"Oh, I do wonder what he will be like!" Rosie said when Maida returned with the information that *skepticism* was not believing in things other people believed in. "There was a time when I just used to hate to have company come to the Little House. But now I feel as though we were living in a story book. There's only one more wonderful thing can happen—and that's to get a fairy godmother down here."

"I don't care what this Mr. Robert Hood is like," Silva said firmly, "he can't be as nice as Mr. Lafayette." She turned to the unconscious Mr. Lafayette and said directly at him in English, "No, he can't possibly be as nice as you are—you perfect angel darling!"

Mr. Lafayette, realizing that he was being addressed, turned his innocent eyes in Rosie's direction.

"Pardon!" he asked.

There was a shout of laughter. No one

but Maida had enough French to make explanation, but she made that explanation rapidly. Mr. Lafayette arose and bowed a very low bow, his plump hand over his heart.

During the week, however, there was very little talk of the mysterious Mr. Hood—the children were so absorbed in the first chapter of the *Adventures of the Big Eight*.

Tuesday morning they spent, each of them, composing a first adventure,—*The Opening of the Little Shop*. The next morning each read his chapter aloud. All the chapters were very brief—too brief, Bunny said at once. Some were only a page.

The children voted that Maida's and Dicky's and Silva's were the best. For one reason Maida—who, because she had had to write letters all her life, expressed herself with great facility—produced a chapter three times longer than any other. And then, she told her story from the point of view of a person inside the shop waiting for things to happen. On the other hand, Dicky's account, though much briefer, had a quality that the children very much liked. He wrote from the point of view of a person outside the shop, watching what was going on—the view indeed of a little lame boy, taking care of a baby sister in a second-story room, while his mother worked all day to earn their living. But what the Big Eight could not understand was how Silva, who was not there at all, could write so interestingly about it.

"Silva used her imagination!" Bunny said. She went on to explain that often the most vivid literature was written by people who had not seen the things they described; only imagined them.

"Now which of these shall we choose for our first chapter?" Bunny asked.

A long discussion followed. Some were for Maida's chapter; some for Dicky's. They all liked parts of other chapters. Then suddenly—Rosie it was—had a brilliant idea.

"Why can't we use parts of them all?" she asked, "for this first chapter?"

"We might divide the chapter in two," Arthur suggested. "You see Maida has written her chapter like one who's inside the shop and Dicky like one who's outside it."

"And we could add sentences here and there," Harold suggested "from the others."

Murmurs of approval or of question greeted these ideas.

Bunny said: "Now children, this is your book, and you must make all the important decisions. Let's vote on this matter."

The vote to adopt Rosie's and Arthur's suggestions was unanimous. Then Bunny herself read all the compositions again. The Big Eight picked sentences and paragraphs here and there; put them where they thought they would most appropriately go.

"What I can't understand," Arthur Duncan said, "is how people make their compositions so long. I can write a few sentences and then I'm through.

It was mainly to answer his question that Bunny talked. And to illustrate what she meant, she acquainted them with some strange terms. "Atmosphere" was one of these. "Characterization" was another. "Dialogue" was a third. "Color" was a fourth. But that morning she spoke particularly on "atmosphere." And she told them how a writer by putting a word here, a phrase there, or a sentence yonder, built up a quality in the book by which you felt yourself absolutely to be in the place she described; and yet you could not put your finger on any one paragraph in the writing which gave you that feeling.

To illustrate this, she read them the first scene from Shakespeare's *Hamlet*.

Before reading, however, she distributed pencils and paper among them. And then she described to them the situation in which *Hamlet* finds himself when the play opens—his father, the king of Denmark but a few months dead and his mother married to his father's brother. She told the Big Eight that this scene occurs just before daybreak on the ramparts of the royal palace. She asked them to try and note down on their paper first the phrases which described that hour; and then all the phrases which made you realize what the place was like in which this scene occurred.

The discussion that followed was highly exciting. Curiously Tyma's observations were the most full. He noted all the things that had to do with the hour; Bernardo's, " 'Tis now struck twelve." Later his, "Well, good night!" Francesco's two speeches, "Give you good night." Marcellus's, "Twice before and jump at this dead hour."

None of the others quoted more than two phrases and some only one. Several wrote down, "Look, the morn in russet mantle clad," although they made curious spellings of "russet" and "mantle."

Bunny said that as long as this problem of "atmosphere" interested them, she would read every day for a week passages in books in which she thought the "atmosphere" was well managed. She asked them to be on the look-out in their reading for such examples. Later perhaps they would read their books from the point of "characterization."

"Now," she concluded, "we are all tired. And tomorrow if you'd like, we will talk over what the next adventure is to be."

"Oh, can't we talk about it now!" Dicky pleaded.

But Bunny only smiled. "Not any more today," she decided firmly.

True to her promise, she permitted them to talk the second chapter over the next day. The children finally decided that the next real adventure was the Halloween party in the Little Shop. Bunny asked them to search their memories for the details of that party. As fast as these details came, she jotted them down on a black-board which she had brought from upstairs. Then after every possible memory was evoked, they talked over the order in which these ideas should be presented. In the end they worked out a definite plan. The children copied this skeleton chapter into their blank books.

"Remember," Bunny said, "you have a whole week in which to write your chapter. Now if in the meantime, any of you get stuck or want help, do come to me, because of course there's nothing interests me so much as writing."

But Bunny did not wait for them to come to her. At various times, she managed to talk alone with each one of the Big Eight in turn. Maida, she discovered, had written her chapter that afternoon. Dicky had finished his the next day. The others all admitted to a dread of beginning. But after they had their talk with Bunny, they became highly excited. Laura and Silva and Arthur went immediately to their rooms. Tyma and Harold and Rosie delayed longest. Indeed Saturday morning Rosie had not written her chapter Bunny proposed that they two take a long walk together early Saturday afternoon. When they returned Rosie dashed to her room and was not heard from for long over an hour.

The next day, the Big Eight read all their second chapters.

After they had finished their discussion of them Bunny read the first chapter of her *Little Tourists in the Southwest*.

The children applauded it.

"Oh how beautiful it is!" Maida said in a trembling voice. "I'll tell you one thing—my next chapter's going to be better. It gives me so many ideas."

"I'll tell you another thing," Dicky said grimly. "My next chapter's going to be longer."

Suddenly it was Friday night again, and they were all waiting for Billy Potter and the new guest. What would he be like, again and again they asked each other. They had expected that Mr. Lafayette would be a huge black giant of a man and he had proved to be—they had all accepted Laura's description—a "robin red-breast." They had expected Miss White to be a middle-

MR. HOOD ARRIVES

aged, white-haired, eye-glassed "motherly" looking woman, and she had proved to be just like a little girl.

"Well, it doesn't make any difference what we think he will be like," Laura said, "he will be different. So let's all say what our idea of him is. My idea is that he's a regular school-master-looking person. And I hope we're going to like him."

"Very tall and very thin with gray whiskers and a lot of hair," Rosie said. "And I think we're going to like him."

"Very fat and round with no whiskers and a bald head," Arthur said. "And I believe we're going to like him."

"An old, old man with a long white beard," Silva said, "looking like a—a—a clever Santa Claus. And I know we're going to like him."

"A very strict person with a stern voice —like a man who has been in the army," Tyma said. "And I'm *sure* we're going to like him."

"All tanned and sunburned—like somebody who has lived out-of-doors all the time," Maida said. "Yes, I expect to like him."

"Very thin and delicate—looks like an

invalid," Harold said. "But I bet he'll be pleasant."

"I haven't even thought of him," Laura said. "But won't it be awful if we don't like him, when we like Mr. Lafayette and Bunny so much? We must never let him guess it, though."

But the man who emerged from the bus, close on Billy Potter's heels that Saturday night, was like no one of these descriptions.

"Wasn't it funny that it never occurred to us that he might be *handsome!*" Rosie said to Maida that night.

"Or *young*," Maida answered.

"Or so *gay*," Laura added.

"We all thought he was going to be nice," Silva recalled, "because Mr. Lafayette and Bunny are so nice."

"But none of us thought he'd be nice in that way," Rosie declared.

"Or in so many ways," Maida reinforced her.

In the meantime the boys were carrying on just such conversation, though in quite different terms.

"Gee, he's a peach!" Arthur began.

"Some guy, believe me!" Harold took it up.

"Wasn't that a great yarn he told Billy about the trip on that scientific ship into the Sargasso Sea?" Arthur went on. "And I heard him tell Mr. Lafayette he'd been in the Arctic Ocean."

"I'll say so," Tyma agreed. "Made me want to run away to sea. And then when he talked about Africa, it made me want to run away to——"

"——run away to land," Harold finished for him.

"I feel just as though I'd been in a dream this evening," Dicky said with a distracted air.

Mr. Hood was young. He was handsome; a slim blade of a figure on which long, powerful muscle was tautly packed, and a thin, tanned, dark face in which a fine spirit glowed. He was extremely gay. And he was full of thrilling adventures.

"Golly, isn't it going to be great mealtimes in this place with him at the table?" Arthur concluded.

And at the same time, "If any more interesting people come to this house," Rosie was saying sleepily, "I don't know what I shall do."

But in the morning, when the children

came downstairs for breakfast, they paused to have a whispered conference in the Map Room.

After the good-mornings, Rosie began timidly, "Mr. Hood, we call Monsieur La Flayosc—Mr. Lafayette, and we call Miss White—Bunny. Do you mind if we give you a nickname?"

"I'd like it very much," Mr. Hood answered. "I shall consider it a compliment. What is it?"

"Robin Hood!" Rosie answered, smiling and blushing brilliantly.

CHAPTER VIII

ROBIN HOOD REMAINS

ARTHUR DUNCAN'S prophecy came true. The talks at mealtimes were so thrilling that Granny Flynn and Mrs. Dore were always having to come in after they had finished eating, to shoo the children out of doors. For the first two or three days, the Big Eight tagged Robin Hood everywhere he went. That involved a great deal of tagging, because the first thing he did was to explore the entire neighborhood. It was thrilling to go with him because he was always discovering wonders in what had become commonplaces in the existence of the Big Eight. The moraine, for instance! They sat down on rocks in a circle about him, while he described to them the ice age, the erosion of the earth's surface which the ice-cap had accomplished; the rocks it had left in its wake.

When the Big Eight took him into

Silva's cave, Robin Hood launched forth into a description of the famous caves of the world. The Mammoth Cave in Kentucky; the Luray Cavern in Virginia; the Altamura Caves of Spain; Miramar in Cuba; the grottoes of the Bermuda Islands. "And many of the Bermuda Caves were discovered by boys," he concluded.

The story of the enterprising boys of Bermuda so thrilled them that the Big Eight embarked on a search for a second cave on the Westabrook place. A two days' hunt produced nothing but conversation, however.

After dinner the whole group, including Bunny, Mr. Lafayette and Billy Potter, surrounded Robin Hood, demanding adventures and asking questions about those adventures.

It was a thrilling evening; for before Robin Hood would describe any place he had seen, it had to be looked up on the map or the globe. And when he began a fresh story, he was always very careful to ask the children questions to see how much they remembered of the last one. In turn, each of his auditors had to describe the geographical locations in reference to surrounding countries, oceans, rivers, big cities.

One night, he proposed that he help Arthur make a big map of the county in which the Little House was situated. All the next day those two worked on it. Watching the proceedings, the others became fired by their enthusiasm; asked if they could make a map too. Presently the Big Eight were sitting round the big living-room table, all working at small maps that duplicated Arthur's big one.

Occasionally Robin Hood dropped an interesting historical fact about the county. And Arthur always said, "Oh, let's mark that spot on the map!"

"Well, why not read the history of the county," Robin Hood said suddenly one day. "Then we can make this map a historical one."

That suggestion thrilled Arthur.

Robin Hood possessed himself of all the books in the library which bore on the history of Satuit. The next morning he began working out for them the history of Massachusetts from the time the Pilgrims landed.

This was so long a story that it ran on from day to day; and their maps grew with it.

Robin Hood developed two other accomplishments. One had to do with riddles. He could ask the most perplexing riddles. He seemed to know an infinite number. Like all children, the Big Eight very much enjoyed riddles—enjoyed them so much in fact that finally every morning Robin Hood wrote one on the living-room black-board. Sometimes the Big Eight solved it in a minute. Sometimes they worked over it at intervals all day.

After a while, however, Robin Hood ran out of riddles and substituted problems. There was never more than one, but it was always a fascinating question which involved a pair of boys or girls, or both— working out the area of a play-room they were building; or the difference in exchange in money in a foreign country in which they were traveling; or the time involved in motoring at so many miles an hour across a desert; in walking at a given pace up a high mountain; or sailing at so many knots an hour across a broad ocean; or the rate of interest on a fortune that had just been left them; or the reduction into money of a vast treasure found on a desert island.

"These are the greatest problems I ever tackled," Arthur said one evening. "Almost always you go traveling when you start one."

Robin Hood's third accomplishment appeared later. One day he said, "I'm not going on any walks today because I have decided that I must do a water-color of that little bit of woodland out there near the moraine. The autumn coloring is very paintable."

"Oh, can you paint pictures?" Nesta exclaimed in an awed tone.

"I not only can but do," answered Robin Hood smiling down on her.

"May we go?" everybody asked.

"Certainly," Robin Hood acceded. He emerged from his room presently, carrying a big, flat box of japanned tin under one arm; an easel and a stool under the other. In a high state of excitement, the children tagged him. He set up his paraphernalia on a spot which, apparently, it took him a long time to choose. Then he began to paint. The children watched, fascinated.

"Oh, I wish I knew how to paint," Rosie sighed wistfully.

"I'll show you how," Robin Hood said calmly.

"Oh, would you?"

"Certainly—any one who wants to learn."

"Oh, I'd just love it," Maida echoed Rosie.

"And I," declared Laura. "I've always wanted to paint."

Silva said nothing, but a sort of ecstatic trembling passed over her slight figure.

"You boys don't seem to be so excited about it," Robin Hood remarked.

"Well, I'd like to know something about painting," Arthur answered a little hesitantly, "because I think this would help me in coloring maps, and I'd rather make maps than anything else."

"It certainly would," Robin Hood agreed.

On one side of Robin Hood, Harold studied the beginnings of the picture; on the other side Tyma studied it.

"I've never wanted to paint," Harold said, "but if the rest of the gang's going to take it up—well, I'll try anything once."

"Same here," Tyma echoed him.

The next afternoon the Big Eight gathered round the big table in the living room. At each place, they found a sketching pad, pencils, and what Rosie described with satisfaction as a "fat" rubber. They were, Robin Hood told them, all to try to sketch the bunch of leaves rising from the shallow dish in the center of the table. He would give them no directions; just said, "Start and see what you can do."

After they had got under way, however, Robin Hood went from one to the other, making suggestions—and he made a great many. To one after the other he said, "Turn your paper on the other side and start all over again. Let me see how you begin." Then, "No, try to outline the whole effect first—like this. See?"

Silva was at the end of the line. When Robin Hood looked at her drawing, he kept complete silence for a moment.

Then quietly, he spoke. "That's very nice indeed, Silva. Very very nice!"

There was a strange note in his voice.

Maida alone seemed to catch that note. She looked up quickly. Something in his expression interested her. She jumped from her chair and ran round to see what Silva had produced.

Silva had not only, long before the rest, finished her sketch of the leaves, but she had coloured them from Robin Hood's box of paints which lay near her on the table. Silva's drawing was very different from the others. It was, Maida decided, not so— well, the only thing she could think of was —not so black; the lines not so dug into the paper. And somehow Silva had put on the color very differently from any of the others——

It seemed to Maida as she looked at Silva's leaves that they actually fluttered.

CHAPTER IX

HALLOWEEN

IT was getting towards the end of October. One morning at breakfast, Bunny said as usual in French, "How are we going to celebrate Halloween?"

Before any one could answer Mr. Lafayette demanded, "What is Halloween?"

Before answering Bunny, the Big Eight made a concerted effort to explain what Halloween meant. The explanation—a patchwork of French, to which all contributed a phrase or two—was broken by shrieks of laughter. They could not decide which was funnier—their own efforts to describe this joyous holiday or Mr. Lafayette's effort to pronounce Halloween.

But before they had finished their breakfast food, the conversation had at last come back to the question of the celebration. There did not have to be much discussion of that; for Bunny, it appeared, had secretly been considering the matter. She had a plan. And when she described that plan, the enthusiasm of the Big Eight grew so rapidly that no opposing idea was even suggested.

Bunny's plan was that the Halloween celebration should take the form of a costume party, everyone to appear masked. Moreover, she suggested that they divide themselves into two groups—women and girls; men and boys; and that each of these groups work out their own schemes as to costume, keeping them all secret from the others. Her last suggestion was that the costumes be as nearly as possible in the spirit of the holiday. She illustrated this point by saying that for any one of them to appear as a foreign personage—say, for instance, Napoleon; or in the costume of a foreign people—like, for example, a Chinese mandarin —would be quite inappropriate. However, one could go as George Washington, or Betsy Ross, or a member of the Pilgrim colony or of the Continental Army—or any similar character.

This was Saturday, and Halloween came the following week. Saturday was always a kind of holiday at the Little House—a left-over from the time when the children went to school. No one ever seemed to do on Saturday any of the things that he had been doing all the rest of the week. This day, immediately after breakfast, they separated into two groups. Bunny took the girls into her room. She insisted that Granny Flynn and Mrs. Dore come too. They came willingly enough. Indeed they were quite as excited as the little girls. Mrs. Dore's Irish eyes were gleaming with excitement and Granny Flynn hobbled up the stairs like an energetic Fairy Godmother.

In the meantime, the boys had retreated with Billy Potter, Mr. Lafayette and Robin Hood to the men's ell. From both places came sounds of a prolonged discussion.

For the next five days, the Little House simmered with excitement and secrecy. That afternoon, Bunny took the four girls over to the Big Town, where they spent two hours shopping. That night at dinner, Billy Potter announced, "We men are going to use the attic for our dressing room. And we are going to ask that, between now and the Halloween party, nobody go up there. You girls must promise that now." He went around the wildly curious circle of the table, demanding that each girl say these words after him. "I will not go up into the attic until the party is over." He even exacted this pledge from Bunny, Granny Flynn and Mrs. Dore.

"I have also another suggestion to make," Billy Potter went on. "And that is that on the night of the party, we make our entrances in any way and at any time we wish. We must all be prepared for surprises of every kind."

"Oh yes," Bunny agreed, "that's a lovely idea. And that reminds me of something I want to say. Everybody must make up his mind that all kinds of queer things happen at Halloween parties and that no one of us is to be frightened, no matter what strange sounds he hears or what strange sights he sees."

The girls shivered and giggled.

The boys merely looked important.

"You understand, girls," Bunny repeated fixing a severe eye on them, "that you are not to be frightened—no matter what happens." She repeated with a significant accent, *"No matter what happens."*

Again the girls shivered and giggled.

Again the boys merely looked important.

HALLOWEEN 109

After this announcement, the excitement seemed, if possible, to increase. Once again Bunny took the girls over to the Big Town. And for long intervals, Billy Potter was closeted alone with the telephone in the living room, every door to the room locked. There arose in the Little House at almost any hour of the day, the sound of conferences hissed in thrilling whispers—of doors hastily slammed as members of the opposed groups passed in the hall; prolonged giggles and sometimes shouts of laughter.

The night before the fateful day, the living-room door was locked. After the children had gone to bed, the three men busied themselves there for hours.

Halloween arrived—one of those clear, cold, blue-and-gold autumnal days with a touch of summer's honey at the heart of its noon. Excitement which had kept at a simmer now fairly sizzled. No one of the girls dared to speak to any one of the boys, for fear they would inadvertently betray a secret. No one of the boys dared speak to each other, while the girls were present, for fear they would throw light on certain dark mysteries.

"It seems as if this day would never

pass," Rosie said despairingly once to Laura.

The last of the afternoon, the children spent in spelling matches, hoping to make the time go more quickly. It did go, though not so quickly as they hoped. But presently it was supper time. The children gobbled their food shamelessly. And as soon as the last mouthful had disappeared, they scattered to their rooms.

There came an interval of complete quiet.

Then suddenly all over the second storey, doors began to open softly. Stealthy footsteps stole down the front stairs. Stealthy footsteps stole down the back stairs. The outer doors—the front door, back door, side doors—opened quietly! tried to shut quietly; but often slammed in the wind.

And now, the entire house was wrapped in silence. Every room was lighted, yet nothing seemed actually to stir in the quiet, but the soft breathing of the two babies in the nursery; the loud breathing of Fawn the bulldog, who was apparently suffering from nightmare; and the stretching of Fluff the cat, as, waking up, she sharpened her claws.

Presently the door leading from the kitchen to the dining room opened. Two pairs of footsteps came across the dining room floor in the direction of the living room. In the doorway appeared a pair of figures—witches. They wore voluminous, long, loose robes with long, loose capes and tall, pointed hoods, all of black—masks also of black. Each carried a broomstick in one hand and a big, stuffed cat in the other.

The two witches looked wonderingly about.

Only a few lights were on and these wore dimming jack-o-lantern shades. At one end of the room, however, a blazing fire made a cavern of flame. Maple boughs, standing upright, filled the corners with all the reds and golds of the rainbow; or, crossed, drew arcs of red-and-gold beauty over the fireplace, the windows and doors. From the mantelpiece a row of jack-o-lanterns grinned on the scene. On the tops of bookcases, occasional pumpkins gleamed.

The witches seated themselves on a footstool, one on either side of the fireplace; holding themselves straight, the broom pointed upward in one hand; the cat seated at their feet. They sat there perfectly still, not speaking to each other; their eyes, the only thing about them that moved, surveying the scene through the slits in their black masks.

Presently the front door opened and, as though it had been blown in by the wind, a small figure drifted across the threshold, through the hall and into the room. The figure wore a flowing skirt and cape of orange and gold, the edges cut like the edges of autumn leaves. The cape turned up over the head into a hood, like an autumn leaf. The sleeves ended in saw-toothed edges like autumn leaves.

The Autumn Leaf floated over to a couch and sat down.

Nobody spoke. For a while the silence was like death.

And now another outside door opened; another visitor arrived—a tall figure with a golden pumpkin—very large—for a body; and another golden pumpkin—much smaller —for a head. Green arms and legs emerged from the golden body. A green cap sat on the golden head. The Pumpkin bowed—a very fat bow—to the company; then tried to sit down. But not being able to manage sitting down, he arose abruptly.

A faint giggle thereupon came from the

HALLOWEEN

Autumn Leaf. The taller of the Witches sniffed faintly.

Still no one spoke.

And now doors were opening everywhere. Visitors were arriving from every direction. Autumn Leaves—one, two, three, four—joined the first Autumn Leaf on the couch. A second tall figure, as rotund as the Pumpkin—only his beautiful scarlet and yellow coloring proved him to be an apple—entered the room.

The Apple bowed fatly also, first to each of the Witches; then to each of the Autumn Leaves; then to the Pumpkin. The Pumpkin bowed to the Apple. They tried to sit down on a couch together, but immediately collided—exactly like two bubbles. Fortunately, unlike bubbles, they did not put each other out. They arose with great dignity, bowed again to each other and to the company; remained standing.

All the Autumn Leaves giggled. The smaller of the two Witches choked and wiped her eyes.

The Pumpkin and the Apple stared haughtily at the gigglers. They stalked with great dignity into opposite corners, where they folded their arms over their globular chests and glowered silently at each other. In their turn, the Autumn Leaves subsided to quiet and the Witches became silent again.

Yet not a word was spoken. The room was very still, waiting——

Suddenly outside arose a blood-curdling yell. Another followed and another until the Little House seemed to rock with the clamor. The Autumn Leaves jumped, and squeaking like a crowd of frightened mice, clutched each other. Then hastily they separated and tried to look as though they had neither started nor squeaked.

The front door flew open and through the hall poured into the room a group of pirates.

A motley and villainous crew they were! They seemed many at first, but they were really only five. Jetty beards and mustaches intensified red gashes of mouths; shaggy eyebrows increased the ferocity of black caverns of eyes. Blood-stained shirts turned away from tawny necks and great gold earrings dangled from ear-lobes. High boots came almost to the belts in which were stuck a dangerous array of old-fashioned

HALLOWEEN 115

knives and pistols. Broad leather hats or high-colored bandannas covered heads.

The leader bore a frightful scar on the left cheek, beginning just beside his nose, meandering down his face and onto his neck. He wore no mask, but over one eye hung an enormous black patch. The other eye gleamed fiercely from a smear of black-and-blue bruise. He pointed a pair of pistols into the room.

"Hands up!" he commanded, "Blanchemain the Pirate and his gang demand your surrender. Hand over all jewelry and money."

All the maskers—the two witches, the five Autumn Leaves, the Pumpkin and the Apple—jumped to their feet; stood with hands well over their heads.

Blanchemain's gang started—one at one end of the room; a second at the other; two in the middle—to search the company. Blanchemain himself continued to stand in the doorway, his pistols leveled.

But Blanchemain's gang proved to be most unusual pirates. They all had leathern bags hanging at their belts. And instead of stripping the jewels from their victims—although that would have been ex-

tremely difficult because nobody wore any—
they *presented* these victims with jewels.

From the leather pouches emerged magnificent necklaces, bracelets, rings set with white, green, red, blue, yellow stones. They might have been diamonds, emeralds, rubies, sapphires, topazes; then again, they might have been *glass*. The necks of the Autumn Leaves and the Witches were soon hung with necklaces, their wrists wound with bracelets; their fingers covered with rings. The Pumpkin and the Apple were decorated with wrist-watches and tie-pins.

Finally Blanchemain put his pistols back into his belt.

"Now masks off!" he ordered.

The masks came off in a flash, Granny Flynn, who was the short fat Witch, saying to Mrs. Dore, who was the tall, slim one, "I was frightened mesilf."

The Pumpkin and the Apple, who turned of course into Robin Hood and Mr. Lafayette, admitted that they had found their part in the masquerade hot work.

The five Autumn Leaves—who changed, of course, into Bunny and the four girls— were much interested in the loot which the pirates had distributed among them. They oh-ed and ah-ed over them; compared them; changed them about to more becoming combinations. And the Pirates, who became of course the four boys, led by Billy Potter, were still very much thrilled by their pistols and cutlasses. For a while everyone milled about the room, laughing and talking with everyone else; examining costumes and explaining how they had kept so many secrets.

Suddenly Laura screamed. "Oh my goodness, look at that!"

They all turned toward the window. There, a gigantic pumpkin was glaring at them out of great eyes; one yellow, one red. Huge black teeth grinned at them.

"Who is it?" everybody asked.

"Oh, it's *Billy!*" Rosie exclaimed, hastily glancing over the group.

The children dashed out of the house and chased the lantern, bobbing on a stick, until they finally caught it—and brought back the panting Billy.

Order restored itself in the Little House.

"And now," Robin said, "we are going to play some of the Halloween games. But to do that, we must—"

He was interrupted by a knock on the front door.

Everyone turned in surprise. Maida started toward the door. But before she could open it, Robin Hood called in a surprised tone, "Come in!"

The door opened and the strangest and most beautiful little figure appeared. An elf surely! It was little and slender as a child. It wore a long coat of green velvet, ending in slashed fringes. Under the fringes appeared shoes fantastically curved up at the toes. The hair, falling from under a close little red cap, was like a shower of fairy gold. One hand was tightly closed.

The figure advanced steadily into the room.

The Pirates maintained their position; but the Witches and the Autumn Leaves steadily retreated. Granny Flynn crossed herself. "It's one of the little people," she muttered. When Granny said "little people," the Big Eight knew she meant fairies. The figure took up a position in front of the fireplace.

"I came from elfland," it said in a high, thin, chanting voice. "I bring you greetings from fays and fairies and elves. And they asked me to distribute among you this fairy gold."

HALLOWEEN

A little hand opened and a shower of golden coins flew through the air. The Autumn Leaves and Pirates scrambled for them. They proved to be tiny flakes of golden paper.

"This fairy money will bring you luck—" the voice went on.

"Oh, it's *Bunny!*" Silva exclaimed.

Bunny laughed and swept the mask from her eyes. The children surrounded her in a flurry of questioning.

"When did you slip away?" and "How did you make this costume without our knowing it?" and "Where did you dress?" "How did you know how an elf looked?" And last of all from Mrs. Dore, "How did you know Irish fairies wore green coats and red caps?"

And now they were ready for the Halloween games. And games they played until they were all exhausted. Bobbing for apples in a tub full of water—throwing apple peel over the shoulder to find the initial of the future spouse—walking down the cellar stairs backward with a mirror in one hand and a candle in the other—biting at an apple, suspended from a string fastened to the ceiling.

"Remember what fun we had in the Little Shop, Maida," Rosie said, "at the Halloween Party last year?"

"Don't you remember how Timmie Doyle fell into the tub when we were bobbing for apples?" Dick said, "And don't you remember that Molly had brought a set of clothes for him to put on because she said she knew he'd fall into something?" Harold said.

"Don't you remember he always fell into mud-puddles?" Laura said.

"Don't you remember how he always called them *pud-muddles?*" Arthur said.

It was half-past ten before the Big Eight went to bed; but for the first time in their lives, they were almost willing to go.

CHAPTER X

NOVEMBER

NOVEMBER flew by on wings. The weather kept miraculously clear and warm; the children were out-of-doors as much as possible. On the other hand—to their frequently and emphatically expressed regret—there was no snow, and every day some one of them was sure to say, "Oh if we could only skate or coast!"

At that, however, life was very thrilling. The *Adventures of the Big Eight* was growing steadily. Now there were four chapters of a reasonable length. However, try as they would, the young authors never could make their chapters a quarter as long as the "Little Tourist" chapters. The four chapters had been copied in careful typewriting, by their composers. Bunny always opened with a reading the sessions in which they talked over a new chapter or their re-written last chapters. Sometimes this reading was only a paragraph. Sometimes it was a chapter straight out of the middle of a book. Sometimes it was a short story.

At first, these readings illustrated that mysterious thing which Bunny called "atmosphere." It seemed a long time before the children could understand what Bunny meant by "atmosphere." But when she asked them to bring their discussions, paragraphs, or sentences from their own reading which made them see and feel the places they were reading about, they discovered that they were beginning to know what "atmosphere" meant.

After that, they discussed an equally puzzling but equally interesting problem—"characterization." "Characterization" was even harder to understand than "atmosphere." It was the method, Bunny explained, by which authors made people in books seem real—like people in life.

For characterization, Bunny read to them Kipling's *Puck of Pook's Hill*.

Here was not only characterization but atmosphere too!

Bunny called their attention to the suddenness with which Puck appeared at the beginning of each story, the cleverness with which he disappeared at the end, how varied was Kipling's description of this magic happening which, after all, had to be the same every time.

Puck of Pook's Hill not only sent the children to the maps, but to the dictionary and the encyclopedia. Bunny had to look up all sorts of historical references for the Big Eight.

Bunny happened to say once that there was a sequel to *Puck of Pook's Hill—Rewards and Fairies.* "After we finish the first book, we'll read that, if you like."

The Big Eight told her by a round of applause that they *would like.* "I wish there were a hundred sequels!" Silva said.

Communication with Mr. Lafayette was growing every day more easy. At first, though, it had seemed that it would never grow less difficult. But both Mr. Lafayette and Robin Hood got into the habit of relating their experiences at the table; and they talked in French. It was not to be endured —missing these extraordinary stories. At the end of two months, it was surprising how much they got of them. Somehow it had become a rule that everybody among them should talk French at the table. Mr.

Lafayette insisted that whenever he used a word that was not understood—no matter by whom—he was to be stopped and questioned. The children comprehended in a general way a great deal more of his talk than they could have exactly translated. Yet every day now they acquired new words. Sometimes the Big Eight actually dropped a French phrase, or a French word, when they were talking with each other.

Mr. Lafayette was an extraordinarily cheerful influence in the house; for often, at twilight, he sat down at the big piano and played and sang for long intervals. As though it sounded a fairy spell, the first note of his beautiful baritone brought the children from all over the house to his side. He knew a great many folk-songs that were not in the French books—songs which have been sung from time immemorial by the French people. Gradually the Big Eight learned these; joined with him when he sang. He still worked hard with Harold and Dicky, who were determined to learn how to play the piano. Occasionally the others tried to thump out a tune, but they were not nearly so interested, and for that reason naturally not nearly so successful, as the two boys. Dicky and Harold actually developed an ambition to play a duet together before the new year.

Just as Mr. Lafayette every day grew more and more interesting, Robin Hood grew more and more interesting. Every morning after breakfast habitually the group gathered about him for stories. And now it had become a thrilling experience to whirl the great globe in the map room until they found the exact geographical point at which his adventure started. And sometimes, through so many oceans did that story move, at so many ports did it stop, over so many rivers and mountains did it pass, that they seated themselves about the big globe, tracing on it every step of the way.

Sometimes Robin Hood made allusions to books which described these countries. By a lucky chance, those books were always in the library of the Little House. Instantly the entire Big Eight would stampede to the book room, but although none of them read all the books, most of them read an occasional one. Over first possession of many of these books there was no argument—perhaps only one would be interested. But over others there often arose a dispute so violent that Robin Hood had to devise a scheme of drawing lots to decide the order in which they should be read.

A reference to Stewart White's *African Camp Fires* immersed the Big Eight in the jungle for a fortnight. A reading from Wilhjalmur Stefansson's *The Friendly Arctic* shot them at once to Polar seas. A stop, during one of Robin Hood's tales, at Holland almost produced a riot as to who should first get *Hans Brinker or the Silver Skates*. The boys were ready to engage in a pitched battle for the possession of *The Man-Eaters of Tsavo,* and the girls, though not physically so violent, were quite as argumentative when it came to *Heidi.* They had all, long ago, read *Seven Little Sisters* and *Each and All,* but now—with the greatest enthusiasm—they re-read them. Tyma discovered in one corner of the library a file of old-fashioned-looking books, uniform in size and binding. He brought them that night to the big table.

"The Rollo books!" Billy Potter exclaimed, picking up one of them. "I haven't seen the Rollo books for years. I read them all when I was a shaver. How do you like them, Dicky?"

"Pretty well," Dicky said. "They tell you a lot about places you'd like to see. If only Rollo wasn't such a teacher's pet, and if Uncle George wasn't such a smarty-cat!"

On the top shelves of the library, the children suddenly discovered, were books of exploration, discovery and travel of a highly grown-up order. It was impossible to read most of them; they were too difficult. Occasionally though Robin Hood read from them a paragraph or a part of a chapter. And always the illustrations were thrilling. The pictures particularly fascinated Arthur. Sometimes at night, he sat barricaded behind high piles of thick volumes. Ever he seemed to think he would get through all of them before bed-time; but he never once accomplished this. Altogether in the Little House—what between Bunny and Robin Hood—there seemed to be a great deal of talk about books. But perhaps that came about because no one felt obliged to read them or to talk about them.

However, all the afternoon, the Big Eight stayed out-of-doors, and all day Saturday.

Robin Hood interested the Big Eight in the signs which showed the on-coming of winter. He never failed to call attention to them—the dying down of the flowers; the changing colors in the leaves; the hardening of the earth; the paling of the skies; the flights—this was a daily and thrilling occurrence—of birds headed south; the shortening of the days; even the slight change in position of that spot in the western horizon through which the sun sank; the gradual march towards the zenith of the winter constellations.

Robin Hood continued to paint out-of-doors a great deal. Some of the group would follow his example with an effort to sketch. But now none of them, except Silva and occasionally Maida or Arthur, attempted to paint. Silva always took her position at Robin Hood's side; painted as long as he painted.

Robin Hood seemed as much interested in her work as in his own. He showed her how effects were obtained. Sometimes after this friendly criticism, Silva would tear up her half-finished painting and begin all over again. The drawing was faulty, the coloring blurred and yet somehow, Silva had a way of making you not only see the thing she painted, but feel it.

Thanksgiving came.

"It seems so strange," Rosie said a little plaintively to Laura once, "not to be looking forward to your vacations—Thanksgiving, or Christmas."

"Of course!" Laura answered, "not going to school, we have vacation all the time. I never thought I'd ever be as lucky as that. Yet I sort of miss looking forward to a vacation too."

"Isn't it all wonderful though!" Rosie commented after a pause.

"Sometimes," Laura answered, "I'm so afraid that I'm dreaming and somebody will pinch me and wake me up, that I don't know what to do."

The Thanksgiving dinner was, the children insisted, the most entertaining they had ever known. Perhaps that was because they had so much to do. It was not so much a Thanksgiving dinner as a Thanksgiving party. For the parents came for over the week-end—Mr. and Mrs. Lathrop; Mr. and Mrs. Brine; Arthur Duncan's father; Mr. and Mrs. Doyle bringing Timmie and Molly; Mr. and Mrs. Clark bringing Dorothy and Mabel; Mr. and Mrs. Hale bringing the still mischievous Betsy.

The Big Eight had to double up to make

room for all these guests. Two boys slept in one room in the men's ell; two girls in one room on the girls' floor. Extra servants came from Mr. Westabrook's Boston house to help.

All the children assisted, however, in the preparation of this dinner. It was a very busy time with everybody. For a week before, they all worked with their water colors, producing, under Robin Hood's supervision, charming little place-cards for the table. Over these cards turkeys meandered —a little lamely perhaps—but in great numbers. And all Thanksgiving morning, while Bunny, Mr. Lafayette, Robin Hood and Billy talked or walked with the parents, the Big Eight, each with an apron tied around his neck, peeled potatoes; cracked nuts; washed cranberries, celery, salad, fruit; removed the seeds from the grapefruit; pinked the edges of the rind, and helped set the table.

Oh what a dinner it was!

"I suppose I shall be hungry again before I die," Maida said when they arose from the dinner, "but at this moment I can't really believe it."

CHAPTER XI

CHRISTMAS

DECEMBER borrowed wings from November; only these wings seemed larger and more powerful, for the month did not fly through their lives—it darted. That was strange too, because one day, discussing it, the children said that hitherto December had always been the longest and slowest month of the year.

"I never saw days go as fast as these," Rosie sighed once. "But that's because we have so many things to do, I suppose."

And Arthur, voicing for the boys something that the girls had already said among themselves, remarked, "I guess one reason December always seemed so long was because we were all looking forward to the Christmas vacation."

"But to Christmas itself most," Harold put in.

"Yes, but the vacation was pretty important. It's the strangest thing not to be looking forward to it. But every day's a vacation here."

"And then this year, we're more busy than we ever were," Harold continued, "getting ready for Christmas."

"Yes," Maida agreed. "That's what we girls have been saying. Of course I want it to snow so much I don't know what to do. And yet, I suppose it's just as well that it doesn't snow. Because we'd certainly be out-of-doors all day long, and then what would become of our Christmas? We never were so busy."

Yes, busy they were; busy every one of them. For they had decided that as it was the first Christmas in the Little House, they would celebrate it as grandly as possible. Christmas Eve there was to be a Christmas Tree. Christmas Day there was to be a Christmas dinner.

Dependent on this general plan were of course dozens of other tiny plans—secrets. Each and all were engaged in Christmas-present making. The result was that for long periods, the members of the Big Eight worked quietly, locked in their rooms. However, occasions arose when advice from a mature mind had to be sought. Bunny,

Mr. Lafayette, Robin Hood, and Billy Potter were in consequence the recipients of so many confidences that it was a marvel how they kept them all straight.

But as important as these conspiracies were, they all gave before a mammoth conspiracy in which only the grown-ups were engaged.

Early in December Billy explained that Mr. Westabrook was giving one big Christmas present to the Big Eight, and that that big present must be housed in the barn. He asked the children not to go into the barn after the first of December, and honorably to avoid, as far as possible, looking at the various packages and bundles which would begin to arrive.

Packages and bundles! Billy's eyes twinkled when he said those two words. And his effort to repress a smile was evident to the entire Big Eight. They talked about it afterwards. But when the "packages and bundles" began to arrive, they realized why Billy had been so amused. It was impossible not to see some of them. A pile of lumber is not a microscopic object. It was moreover impossible to remain oblivious to the arrival, early every morning, of a group of workmen or late in the afternoon, to their departure. All kinds of bulky, boxed-up objects began to come by express. Occasionally these were enormous.

Excitement, which as a habitual emotion had since Halloween died in the Big Eight, began to burn again. It flamed and flared until life was one continual blaze of wonder and curiosity.

Of course, among themselves the children discussed this mystery endlessly; commented on the arrival of the strange objects continually.

"*What* do you suppose is going on in the barn?" Arthur would say.

"What *do* you suppose is going on in that barn?" Harold would say.

"What do you *suppose* is going on in that barn?" Tyma would say.

"What do you suppose is going on in that *barn?*" Dicky would say.

Laura confined her efforts to moaning occasionally, "I'm going crazy."

Guesses flew through the air—from a swimming pool to a roller-skating rink; a garage to an aerodrome.

"I know what's going on in the barn,"

Silva said one night, lifting sparkling eyes from *Little Men* which, in her long progress through the Alcott books, she had now reached. "They're putting up a cook stove for us."

The girls—and some of the boys too—laughed.

"Oh, that's such a lovely chapter in *Little Men!*" she explained for the benefit of those who had not read her favorite book. "You see the boys get into the way of not playing with the girls, and so Aunt Jo bought the girls a little cook stove. It was a secret to them until it arrived. And it was a secret to the boys until the girls cooked their first meal on it, and invited them to it. Oh I nearly died of curiosity while I was reading that chapter!"

The work in the barn went on. And all the time, the sound of saws and hammers rang in the ears of the Big Eight.

"One way you look at this month," Arthur said, "it's flying past like a bird. And another way you look at it, it's lasting a hundred years."

Events more maddening and even more unendurable, followed. There came days when Bunny or Mr. Lafayette or Robin

Hood, or two of them or all three of them, would take the Big Eight away for all day. Some of these excursions were for Christmas shopping in the Big Town. Other involved long motor trips through the country and a lunch far away from home. The children were acute enough to realize that they were being taken off so that they would not see something too big to be concealed.

"I dreamed about what they were doing in the barn last night," Arthur said once.

"Oh, what were they doing?" Rosie demanded eagerly.

"They'd turned it into a zoo," Arthur replied laughing. "Oh, it was the funniest dream. It was a zoo like a stable. Lions and tigers were standing about in stalls and monkeys were running all over the walls and ceilings and hanging by their tails from hooks. And there was a big pond in the center with a great boa constrictor in it. I didn't seem to be frightened, though. In my dream I seemed to know that none of these animals would hurt me. Oh yes, I've forgotten the best of all. There was a gang of baby elephants playing leap frog."

"Goodness!" Rosie shuddered. "A boa

constrictor! I hope it isn't going to be that kind of a surprise!"

Though increasingly they longed for Christmas Eve to come, nevertheless the Big Eight had to keep busy. They were, of course, still making Christmas presents. There had to be a discussion in regard to these creations, because they did not want to duplicate gifts for the grown-ups. And after various long talks, they came to the conclusion that the thing to do was to get together one substantial gift for each of them. But what that gift should be—there were as many ideas as there were members of the Big Eight; more sometimes.

In Christmas week Bunny informed them that all their presents should be done up and marked by the day before Christmas.

"There will be a big straw hamper at the foot of the stairs," she explained, "and you can put all your gifts in it."

"Can't we put them on the Tree ourselves?" Maida asked in a plaintive voice.

Bunny seemed to have difficulty in keeping her lips from smiling. "No," she said. "None of you are to see the Christmas Tree until Christmas Eve."

The children groaned. But of course

they smiled, too. For by this time, they knew that the suffering of suspense preceding the revelation of a delightful surprise is the pleasantest suffering they were ever going to endure. However, the last day before Christmas was not as bad as the ten days before. For all the morning, the children gathered Christmas greens and under Bunny's instructions made wreaths from them. They decorated every mantelpiece with bunches of holly and mistletoe; hung at every window wreaths of box, tied with scarlet ribbons.

Inevitably the Big Eight discovered dozens of last things to do. Tying up Christmas packages and marking Christmas tags proved to be a feverish occupation. For an hour afterwards, the bathrooms were filled with children trying to remove ink from face and fingers.

"I don't know how I got any ink behind my ears," Dicky said, "but I managed it somehow. I always seem to think I'm taking a shower bath when I write with a pen."

And then half-way through the afternoon of the day before Christmas—the long longed-for, long hoped-for miracle happened.

CHRISTMAS

Snow came.

Came first in leisurely floating motes, and then in swift, direct flakes; changing gradually to pellets, big as rice and seeming quite as hard, which choked the air; turning finally into what looked—so big, so flat, so dry, so close were the starry flakes—like an endless curtain of the most delicate lace, lowering itself constantly from the gray sky. The tumult outside enormously added to the excitement inside. It seemed to close in on that excitement, to hold it tight and thick. The Big Eight had been busy enough early in the afternoon with the preliminaries of the Christmas dinner. But in the twilight —the grown-ups having immediately after dinner shut themselves up in the barn—the children were left to their own devices. They sat about the fire-place in the living room; or played games feverishly; or talked disjointedly; or made an effort to read; or tried for the second time to talk; or engaged in a half-hearted spelling match; or tried for the third time unavailingly to talk. At intervals, somebody was sure to say, "What *do* you suppose is going on in that barn?"

Finally they went upstairs and changed into their party clothes. Never was supper such a failure. No one could eat. Everyone was pining with curiosity. But no one asked questions. And then at the end, the grown-ups disappeared in the direction of the barn.

At seven o'clock exactly, they returned. "Now form in line, everybody," Billy directed. "Granny, you march with me. Mrs. Dore, you march with Mr. Lafayette. Bunny, you march with Robin Hood. And you children come two by two behind us.

Somebody turned the radio on and to a burst of gay music, the procession started. It wound through the four rooms which connected the house with the barn. For a while the taller grown-ups, at the head of the line, obscured the view. But as they entered the wide doorway, they parted and took positions on either side. Unimpeded, straight ahead, gleaming with fairy lights in red, blue, green, shining through films of gold and silver tinsel, each branch dangling a vivid ornament, towered—a perfect cone in shape, and ending in a needle-pointed silver ornament—the Tree almost touched the ceiling. But above it, suspended from a wooden rafter, a flying angel with arms outstretched seemed to command it to grow no higher. Under it lay huge piles of presents.

The children broke and ran—stopped and stared. Then with a common impulse all—grown-ups and children alike—clasped hands and danced around the tree.

"I thought the tree at the Little Shop was the most beautiful one I ever saw," Laura said breathlessly, when the ring broke, "but this is even more beautiful than that."

"It's bigger, you see," Rosie pointed out.

Of them all, Silva and Tyma said nothing. Their eyes were big with wonder though, for they had never seen anything like it in their lives.

And then suddenly, "Why look at the traveling rings on the ceiling!" Arthur exclaimed.

"And the chest weights on the walls!" Dicky exclaimed.

"And that rack of fencing foils," Harold exclaimed.

"And what's that big thing over there in the corner?" Tyma asked.

"I know what that is," Arthur cried at the top of his voice. "It's what they call a horse. Oh, now I know what the surprise is. It's a gym!"

The Big Eight took up Arthur's cry. "A gym! a gym!" they echoed. And again all —grown-ups and children alike—clasped hands and danced around the Tree.

"Oh, what fun we're going to have in a gym!" Harold's clear voice emerged from the confusion. "I'd like to fence. I don't suppose there's any way to learn, though."

Robin Hood asked Mr. Lafayette a rapid question in French.

"I'll teach you," Mr. Lafayette said in French. "All little French boys learn to fence!"

"I fence a little myself," Robin Hood added.

"I'm going to learn to use those—traveling rings, do you call them?" Rosie declared, her eyes sparkling, "just like the ladies in the circus."

"Me for the chest weights!" Arthur declared. "I've got to develop a lot of strength. I'm going to be an Arctic explorer."

"I'm going to do every one of those things," Tyma said modestly.

Billy made explanation. "This gym is, as I told you, Mr. Westabrook's Christmas gift to you all," he concluded. "It was pretty hard keeping it a secret, because we had to put a one-piece furnace in besides disguising all this apparatus. However, we always sent you away for a day when we knew the big things were going to arrive. Now, when the weather keeps us indoors, we'll always have a place for exercise."

"Look!" he interrupted himself in an astounded voice, "if here isn't Santa Claus."

It was true. Santa Claus was bearing down on them. Santa Claus in the gayest of red velvet suits, trimmed with white fur; Santa Claus, white-locked, white-bearded and white-mustached; Santa Claus with a huge pack on his back and a wide smile on his face. Of course the children soon realized that Mr. Lafayette had recently disappeared from their midst. But they politely pretended not to recognize the new arrival. Unfortunately they all talked French to him. However, utterly unembarassed by this error in etiquette, Santa Claus began distributing the gifts, reading the names on the tags with a strong French accent.

CHAPTER XII

TWELVE DAYS OF CHRISTMAS

ON Christmas morning Bunny informed the children that the Christmas holidays really did not end until Twelfth Night and that Twelfth Night occurred just twelve nights after Christmas. By Twelfth Night all the Christmas greens must be taken down or the goblins would get into them. The Big Eight were thrilled by this information. They were delighted to keep this most agreeable of all holidays. Bunny was so entertained by their rejoicing that, after breakfast, she read aloud a story by William Dean Howells about a little girl who so wanted it to be Christmas every day that finally a good fairy granted her that wish. However, the little girl found Christmas every day so monotonous an experience that finally she begged to be let off.

"Twelve days more of Christmas for *us!*" Rosie said after Bunny had finished the story.

TWELVE DAYS OF CHRISTMAS 145

The snow kept up all day Christmas, and when the Big Eight went to bed the air still boiled white.

"Eleven days more of Christmas!" Maida called to the other girls when she waked up the next morning.

"Oh look!" Rosie answered, "the snow's stopped—and the whole world's white!"

Winter sports filled all that afternoon.

Not far from the Litte House was a hill; treeless on top and with a fine slope. The Big Eight trampled down the snow until it was as firm as their amateur efforts could make it. The sleds and double-runners which had come from under the Christmas Tree soon packed the snow to an iron hardness, a glassy smoothness. The Big Eight actually went to bed without being told.

That night came a fall of temperature, a light rain and a sudden freeze.

"Ten days more of Christmas!" Silva called when she awoke the next morning. "Oh, look out your windows, girls," she was commanding in another moment. "The trees are all trimmed with icicles!"

Their coast had turned to a glare of ice and coasting itself to flying. The whole household turned out—even to Mrs. Dore.

Granny Flynn actually consented to go down the hill once on the double-runner.

What a day that was!

"Nine days more of Christmas!" Laura called the next morning.

"Today," Robin Hood suggested at breakfast "we'd better try the skis."

"Oh, I'd forgotten all about the skis," Maida said.

"I hadn't," Arthur Duncan declared, "I've just been waiting for something to be said about those skis."

Skiing was fun too, another kind of fun; in most ways no less entertaining than coasting; and in some ways, more so. As was to be expected, Harold took to skiing as a duck takes to water—as Harold took to every game and sport.

In the speed with which he learned to manipulate the new foot-gear, Arthur proved a close second to Harold. But as to the others—they spent most of their time, face down and skis up, in snow drifts. They laughed so hard at themselves and at each other that sometimes they had actually to be rescued from the drifts in which they threatened to choke to death. For the first few days they returned to the Little House as white as though they had been modeled from snow. Gradually, however, they got what Rosie called the "hang" of the new sport. Suddenly Tyma started to improve. Presently he rivaled Harold.

"Eight days more of Christmas!" Silva called the next morning. "I wonder what we'll do today."

But as it happened the girls coasted alone that day. For after breakfast, "I wonder if we boys could go off on a long hike with you today?" Arthur timidly asked Robin Hood.

"Certainly!" Robin Hood answered. He glanced from the thrilled faces of the boys to the suddenly sobered faces of the girls; seemed to await something. But no one said anything.

"We'll ski across country," he suggested absently.

The party returned full of the most extraordinary stories of their adventures. They were most interested in the marks they had seen in the snow, tiny tramplings of birds and small animals. Robin Hood could read these tracks as clearly as though it were a black writing on a white wall. Here a track indicated mere exploration;

here flight; yonder a fox had stalked a pheasant down the side of a little ravine. The boys followed the claw and pad prints breathlessly, but apparently the pheasant had learned that there was a pursuer on his track and had taken to the trees. Once appeared an area infinitesimally scuffed with conflict, which showed that one bird flight had ended in capture.

"I wish we girls could go on a long hike," Rosie said in an injured voice that evening.

"Oh, they're altogether too long for a girl," Arthur answered in a superior tone. "You'd get tired out before we'd been out an hour."

"I don't know whether I would or not," Rosie answered loftily. "I notice when it comes to anything else, I don't get any more tired than you boys."

"I should love to see those little tracks," Maida said wistfully.

"Seven days more of Christmas!" Maida called the next morning.

The Magic Mirror had frozen, of course, but for a while it was covered with snow. Successive changes in weather had removed the snow from the ice; evened the ice to a satiny smoothness. That day, the skates which had also emerged from under the Magic Tree, were all in use. Rosie, Laura, Harold and Arthur were good skaters. The other four had never had a chance to learn, Maida and Dicky because of their lameness; Silva and Tyma because they never could have afforded to buy the skates.

Great as was the enjoyment of the favored four, it was nothing to that of the less favored four. They tripped and fell; arose, tripped and fell; arose again; tripped and fell again. In fact they tripped and fell all the afternoon long.

That night, too, the Big Eight went to bed without, as Granny said, "having to be rocked to sleep."

"Six days more of Christmas!" Laura called the next morning.

Again the Big Eight engaged themselves with skating.

"Five days more of Christmas!"

More skating.

"Four days more of Christmas!"

On all these days, Tyma, Dicky, and the two girls rushed over to the pond at every opportunity. Maida and Silva learned to skate hand-in-hand. They were a pretty sight; gloved hands interlocked; slender figures swaying from side to side in a beautiful rhythm; eyes turned to jewels and cheeks to blossoms—yes, even Silva's amber skin bloomed with faint roses—by the magician, Wind.

"Three days more of Christmas!"

That day the Big Eight started to make a one-room snow house. In the end, they spent two afternoons on this delightful architecture. In the process they proceeded to make not one room—to be sure it was no larger than a closet—but four. Getting interested in these rooms, they proceeded to make furniture—snow-tables and chairs. Getting interested in their furniture, they proceeded to produce tenants. Before they had finished, each room contained at least one occupant. This person was likely to be a little eccentric in appearance. The clothes were of an ancient cut and much worn, having been brought down from the garret. But on the other hand, this snow-person was extremely genial as to sparkling eyes—they were made from marbles—and expansive smiles—they were evolved from orange-peel teeth. In the living room, there appeared two snow children. They were extremely well behaved, though a little stupid; for they never moved from the seats on which they sat; never took their eyes from that point on the wall at which, from the beginning, they had steadfastly stared. After infinite labor Rosie also produced something that remotely resembled a cradle in which lay an object remotely resembling a baby.

Through the air flew flippant criticisms in regard to the baby. Arthur said it looked more like a kitten than a baby. Harold said that it much more closely resembled a puppy. Tyma declared that if Rosie had not told him that it was a baby, he would have taken it for a fish. Rosie received all these remarks with sparkling smiles. In her own defense, however, she did say that she challenged any one of them to mold out of snow a more quiet or well-behaved baby. Robin Hood wandered out from time to time to see what progress the snow apartment was making.

"I tell you what I'll do with you," he said, "how would you like to build an Eskimo snow house on the hill over by the Magic Mirror? It's so exposed there that if we tamped the snow down hard and left it over night, it would be solid enough in the morning."

"Oh, gee!" Arthur exclaimed excitedly. "Can't we do it now?"

"You mean like those houses you showed us in the book last night?" Tyma asked eagerly.

"It would be great if we could sleep there one night," Dicky said in an electric voice. "With skins on the floor the way you said the Eskimos do."

So great was the excitement among the boys that they stopped work.

"Why can't we go too?" suddenly spoke up the gentle Silva.

"Oh you girls could never stand anything like that," Tyma answered his sister.

"I don't know why we couldn't," Silva answered quietly.

"I don't think you boys are so much stronger than we are," Laura added. "When it comes to doing anything useful, I notice, you always think we're as strong as you."

"I'm sure we could do everything that you do," Maida insisted in an injured voice.

"Well, some time perhaps," Arthur, who

had a way of settling things, answered. "But this first time, I guess we boys better do it alone."

Robin Hood said nothing. Bunny said nothing. But they exchanged glances.

"Two more days of Christmas!" Maida called the next morning.

"Yes and those mean boys are going to make their ice-house today." Rosie answered in an aggrieved tone.

The boys were gone until dusk. With a definite sense of injury, the girls skated and coasted together; made lonely explorations of their snow house.

They listened in silence to the enthusiastic out-pourings of the boys.

"I'm not interested," Rosie commented loftily when they finished. "Let's talk about something else."

"One more day of Christmas!" Silva said mournfully the next morning.

That day of Twelfth Night came—and Christmas was over. With Bunny, Mr. Lafayette, and Robin Hood at their head, the children marched all over the house removing the greens from the mantels and taking the wreaths down from the windows. These greens and wreaths were solemnly burned in the fireplace. The beautiful Christmas Tree, still standing majestically in the center of the Gym, was divested of its tinsel bravery. The bright-colored toys were wound in tissue paper, placed in boxes, and put away for next year's Tree. The Tree itself was dragged from its proud position out into the snow and, because the children could not bear to see it lying there, chopped up and burned in the living-room fire.

"Christmas is gone," Rosie announced in a heartbroken voice.

CHAPTER XIII

A GUESS IN JANUARY

IT was the afternoon after Twelfth Night. The Big Eight had gathered in the Gym.

Outside, it was snowing briskly. On stormy days the children flocked to the Gym. This afternoon they were alone. The grown-ups—and this very rarely happened—were engaged in their own affairs. The Big Eight had been exercising frantically. Now they sat about the broad fireplace which in spite of the addition of a furnace, still remained. A huge blaze filled the big room with a dancing light.

"What a Christmas this has been!" Rosie exclaimed in a low voice.

"You're always saying that when you were in school you looked forward so to your Christmas vacation," Maida accused her, "that you really enjoyed Christmas more. Did you enjoy this Christmas as much?"

"You bet I did," Rosie admitted. "Do you boys miss school?" she asked.

"Yes," Arthur said with emphasis, "I miss it, but it's a *good* miss."

"That's just the way I feel about it," Harold agreed.

"Well, I'd like to ask you," Maida went on impatiently, "would you like to grow up perfectly ignorant, not knowing a single thing?" Her tone was a little defiant and she directed herself to Rosie.

"No," Rosie said. "No. I do want to know something of course. But I don't want to learn it the way you learn it in schools."

"But just think how much we're learning here," Silva put in in her quiet voice.

"Yes," Tyma supplemented her. "We're learning all the time."

"Oh, when you stop to think of that—" Harold started.

"Oh, yes, when you stop to think of that—" Arthur interrupted.

"I never learned so much in my life," Dicky finished for both of them.

"Nor I," agreed Harold. "Or so much of the things I most like."

"Just think of it," Rosie broke in, "we've

A GUESS IN JANUARY

all learned to speak French. Not very well, of course. Still, Mr. Lafayette said the other day tht if we were dropped from an airplane in France, we ought to be able to *get along.*"

"Yes," Arthur added, "and look at the geography we know. Why sometimes I feel as if I'd traveled all over the world. I've heard of places that I never knew about—like the Cameroons in Africa, and——"

"—and those little republics in Europe," Harold interrupted, "San Marino and Andorra."

—"and the Gobi desert," Tyma contributed, "and the dinosaur eggs."

Dicky, who had been very thoughtful, suddenly made a contribution to the conversation. "And think of the arithmetic we've learned."

"Arithmetic!" Arthur repeated, "what do you mean—*arithmetic?*"

"Why, those problems that Robin Hood puts on the blackboard every day," Dicky said. "Of course they're always about very interesting things and people—almost like a story—but they're arithmetic just the same."

"I guess you're right, Dicky," Arthur

agreed. "Now isn't that curious. It never occurred to me that they were arithmetic. But of course they are."

"Yes," Harold contributed, his face lighting up as though a new idea had struck him, "just as all this tracing journeys over the globe is *really* geography. I never thought of it as geography—but of course it is."

"I guess you're right, too," Arthur agreed again. "Isn't it curious I never thought of it as geography either." He paused for a moment and just as in Harold's case, a great light seemed to burst upon him, and he exclaimed, "Well, all the facts we've been looking up about the country for the maps is history in a way. Why, we've been learning history too."

"I know one thing," Harold declared, "I've been learning music."

"I know the same thing," Tyma echoed. "I know I've been learning music too."

"And nobody can tell me that I haven't been learning painting," Silva laughed.

"In fact we've all been learning something," Rosie said. She added uncertainly, "I mean a lot of things."

"Oh, how I dread having the Little School

a shower of sparks made fire-works on their way up the chimney. It was as though that noise exploded something in their minds.

"I've got it," Rosie said in a triumphant voice. "There's no Maida's Little School, and there's never going to be any Maida's Little School. I mean in *that* way. We've been going to school for months. We're going to school now. We're going to Maida's Little School this moment."

The children stared at her aghast. Then all round the half-circle eye met eye. What they read in each other's faces was reflected back in their own—stupefaction, wonder, certainty.

CHAPTER XIV

THE CONSPIRACY

"DO you mean, Rosie," Arthur demanded, "that they've been playing a trick on us?"

"That's exactly what I mean," Rosie declared.

Maida burst into shrieks of laughter. "That would be exactly like my father."

"That's just what's happened," Harold exclaimed excitedly. "Don't you remember how we told him that we hated to go to school? And he got Billy to ask us all the things we disliked about school, and how we'd like them changed?"

"I remember perfectly," Rosie said in a low thrilled voice, "that I said if we could go to school without knowing it, it would be fun."

"Yes, Rosie," Maida said; "and don't you remember you said you wished you could take ether when you went into school, and not come out of it until school was over?"

THE CONSPIRACY

"Did I say that?" Rosie asked—and laughed.

"That's what happened!" Harold said, "Mr. Westabrook made up his mind that he'd send us to school without letting us know anything about it."

"He and Billy planned it together," Laura interrupted.

"They certainly did," said Arthur. "You see how clever they've been about it. First Mr. Lafayette came here. And before we knew it we were studying French."

"Not studying, Harold," Silva demurred, "we've never looked into a single book."

"That's why it's so wonderful," Arthur said with a delighted smile.

"Yes, you see," Maida explained, "from the first we all liked Mr. Lafayette so much—I mean *loved* him so much—that we wanted to learn French so that we might talk with him. Wasn't that a clever thing to do? It's like a lovely April Fools' Day joke."

"Then Bunny came," Harold went on, "and the first thing we knew we were all writing compositions."

"You mean writing a *book!*" Silva corrected proudly.

"Yes, but it was writing compositions just the same," Harold insisted, "although, I will say, I never enjoyed writing compositions and I have enjoyed writing the book."

"Yes, and Bunny reads to us and gets us to read by ourselves," Dicky added.

"—and teaches us spelling," Laura added, "through the spelling matches."

"But what about Robin Hood?" Laura demanded.

Arthur made a despairing gesture in his chair as one who cannot voice all the ideas that come to him. "Robin Hood! *Robin Hood!* Why Robin Hood is teaching us geography and——"

"History," Maida interrupted.

"How to make maps," Arthur started in again.

"How to paint," Silva interrupted.

"And arithmetic," Harold completed the list.

"To think I never guessed!" Maida mourned. "But oh how I've enjoyed it!"

"Don't think you're the only one who enjoyed it, Maida Westabrook," Rosie rebuked her sharply. "There's no one of us who's ever had such a good time and learned

THE CONSPIRACY

so much before, is there?" She turned to the rest of the group.

The Big Eight made swift nods and loud noises of assent.

"I think it's the most wonderful joke I ever heard in my life," Arthur agreed with conviction.

"So do I!" "So do I!" and "So do I!" ran enthusiastically about the circle.

"There's only one thing I'd like to do," Arthur added, "and that's to play a joke on them—I mean Mr. Westabrook and Billy—a joke just as nice as the one they've played on us."

CHAPTER XV

THE CONSPIRACY CONTINUED

THERE were long-drawn "Ohs!" of joy at Arthur's suggestion.

"If we only could," Maida said in a delighted voice. "Oh, how I'd love to play a beautiful joke on my father. He's played so many on me."

"The question is, though," Arthur went on, "what could it be?"

A film of thoughtfulness fell over the circle of excited faces. Everybody pondered.

"We could have some jokes fixed up in his room," Harold said a little uncertainly, "that he'd find when he came back."

"No," Arthur said decidedly, "I don't mean that sort of thing. It's to be a joke like the one he's played on us—something that's so nice when you find it out, that you're glad it's been played on you."

"We might write him a round-robin letter of thanks for the Little School," Rosie suggested, "and put it in his top drawer."

THE CONSPIRACY CONTINUED 167

"That's better," Arthur approved. "Only I wish it wasn't quite so easy as that. I'd like it to be something harder—I mean something that would take longer than just opening a drawer."

"The night he arrived, we might dress up as Blanchemain's gang," Dicky suggested, "and come yelling into the house and present him with the letter, thanking him for the Little School."

"That's not a bad idea," Arthur approved again.

"Oh, I tell you what we might do," suggested Harold, the ingenious, "we might present him with a fake map which we'd pretend was a map of Blanchemain's buried treasure. We'd take him to the spot and dig and there he'd find in a tin box the letter, thanking him for the Little School."

"That's a crackerjack of an idea, Harold," Arthur exclaimed enthusiastically. "Now," he went on, "we've got some good ideas—bringing Blanchemain the pirate into it and his treasure trove, and the pirates' map. But perhaps we can think of something better than this, although we might use all these ideas. Let's talk it over."

The hours that the Big Eight had put in, working out chapters in the *Adventures of the Big Eight,* now stood them in good stead. They began to think of their joke in the terms of a story.

"I wonder," Silva broke out suddenly in her soft little voice, "if we could fool Mr. Westabrook in regard to the map? If we could make it look old?"

"Oh, *gee!*" Arthur exclaimed, leaping to his feet, "that's another great idea, Silva. You *can* make a map look old. Robin Hood was telling me about it the other day. I'll ask him how you do it."

"—so that"—Silva went steadily on, "Mr. Westabrook would think it was really a map that Blanchemain the Pirate had left somewhere."

"It might drop out of an old book," Maida said.

"No, we haven't a book old enough," Arthur settled that.

"Oh, if there was only a secret chamber in the house," Laura moaned, "or a secret stairway between the rooms, or a secret drawer in one of the old desks!"

"It might be in a trunk in the attic," Tyma said.

THE CONSPIRACY CONTINUED 169

"Oh, I know," Maida suggested electrically, "I know! Why couldn't the map be buried too—and just found accidentally?"

"That's it, Maida!" Arthur agreed.

Arthur was excited now, his eyes were blazing. His cheeks had turned a vivid crimson. He looked almost handsome.

"Now," he continued, counting these facts on his fingers, "we're decided on three things. Something to do with the treasure of Blanchemain the Pirate; a map which looks as though it were old; the map to be buried. But—but—" He paused and knitted his brows. "What's the map got to do with the treasure and the letter thanking Mr. Westabrook for the Little School?"

"I've got it," Rosie burst out in a voice almost as excited as Arthur's. "I've got it. We'll have to have two buried things—the map and the letter. The buried map tells where the letter is."

"But if the map tells where the buried treasure is," Arthur pointed out, "we'll have to have something telling where the map is."

"Oh, that's easy," Harold said, *"that's easy.* We'll have a mark cut on a tree, pointing downwards to where the map is buried. We'll take Mr. Westabrook to walk past it. And call his attention to it and wonder what it means."

"But," Tyma interposed, "that mark would have to be cut into the tree over two hundred years ago. In the first place it would have changed its shape during all those years, and in the second place it would have grown up so high that he couldn't see it."

Harold's bright face blanked for a moment. The faces of the Big Eight grew sober.

"We don't have to put the sign on a tree," Tyma himself declared. "We can carve it on a rock. If we start now, we can make it look old by the spring."

"You've got it, Tyma!" Arthur said. "That's the way we can do it!"

He jumped up from his chair and walked round to slap Tyma approvingly on the shoulder.

"One more thing," Arthur added. "We can't have the map or the letter put in a tin box because of course it wouldn't look old. Oh, I *know* what we can do—I know what we can do! It's going to be hard work, but

THE CONSPIRACY CONTINUED 171

we can make a box out of some of the old boards they took from the barn. We'll have to put it together with wooden pegs, the way people of long ago did. And we'll bury it as soon as possible, so that it will look as though it had been in the earth for centuries."

Arthur's voice ran down. His eyes fixed in a kind of perplexity.

"The only thing that I don't particularly like about this plot is that letter," he said slowly. "I wish we could think of something better." He paused, thinking hard —and all the Big Eight kept silent, thinking with him.

Suddenly a flame blazed back of Arthur's eyes. "I've got it!" he yelled exultantly. "I've got it now! The very best thing we can do. Listen!"

The Big Eight listened eagerly while Arthur told them the rest of the plot.

CHAPTER XVI

THE CONSPIRACY CONTINUED

"BUT can we do this all alone?" Rosie asked; "or shall we have to have somebody to help us? I mean—shall we tell Bunny or Mr. Lafayette or Robin Hood?"

There came another of the silences which had marked this conversation, as the children considered—and with a deep intensity —a new aspect of the situation. Then suddenly they all broke out together.

"I don't think we could possibly do it alone," Harold said.

"We must get help about the map and the treasure boxes," Arthur said.

"Besides, we never could keep it from Bunny or Mr. Lafayette or Robin Hood," Tyma said.

"One of them would be sure to guess that something was up," Dicky said.

"I think we'd better tell them," was Rosie's advice.

"We'll all enjoy it so much more, if

THE CONSPIRACY CONTINUED 173

everybody's in the secret," was Laura's opinion.

"I want Granny Flynn to know about it," Maida insisted.

"And Mrs. Dore," said Silva, who never forgot how Mrs. Dore nursed her when— with her broken leg—she first came to the Little House.

"Let's tell them all at supper!" Rosie's black eyes first fired, then blazed with delight.

"Why, there's the first supper bell now!" Harold said. "Would you believe we've been talking such a long time?"

The children rushed up to their rooms and made as quickly as possible the inevitable preparations for supper. Mr. Westabrook had decreed that the boys should put on clean blouses every night, and Granny Flynn had decreed that the little girls should change into fresh frocks. It was always with cheeks shining from hot water and hair glossy from the brush that the Big Eight filed to the supper table. But tonight, there was a special air about them— of an excitement so great that it danced in their eyes and poured out in the continued restlessness of their movements.

"You tell them about it, Arthur," Rosie said as they came through the hall. "You know so much more about maps and things."

"All right," Arthur agreed.

Nevertheless there was an unwonted silence after the Big Eight had taken their places. They kept looking at each other and at Arthur. Laura giggled faintly and then suppressed her giggles.

"What *is* it?" Bunny asked at last. "What are you children up to?"

"We've got something to tell you," Arthur began. Arthur's face was solemn and his voice was so feeble that it sounded like the peep of a chicken. His tone grew in strength as he went on, however, and presently he was talking with his characteristic vigor.

"We've got something to tell you that's very important and very interesting—very interesting to us, I mean. I don't know exactly how to begin. But you see, we were all talking in the gymnasium this afternoon and saying how much we enjoyed living in the Little House, and how much we were learning, and all of a sudden—I can't remember now how it happened——"

"How *did* it happen?" Maida interrupted in a puzzled voice.

"How did *what* happen?" Bunny asked. Her eyes were dancing too and she had caught some of their restlessness from the children.

Arthur paid no attention to Maida's question, but he immediately answered Bunny's.

"Well, all of a sudden we guessed that there never was going to be any Maida's Little School, because there *is* a Maida's Little School. I mean, we guessed that we've been going to school for three months without knowing it."

"We guessed," Rosie put in breathlessly, "that Mr. Westabrook has played a joke on us——"

"A perfectly beautiful joke," Silva interrupted.

"Yes," Rosie agreed, "a perfectly beautiful joke, but a joke just the same."

Bunny clapped her hands like a child. "I knew you'd discover it." She looked triumphantly from Robin Hood's face to Mr. Lafayette's. "Didn't I tell you," she crowed over them, "that these children would find it out!"

"You certainly did!" Robin Hood declared.

Mr. Lafayette looked mystified. Bunny and Robin Hood, alternately interrupting each other, told him rapidly in French what the Big Eight had just revealed. Mr. Lafayette threw back his head and roared his big bass roar.

"But that isn't all," Rosie took up the story. "We want to play a joke on Mr. Westabrook and Billy. It's a nice joke—almost as nice as theirs, though not such a big and important one. And we want you to help us."

"You can," Harold explained; "you helped *them,* so it's perfectly fair for you to help *us.*"

"Perfectly," Bunny agreed, her dimples snapping in and out of her cheeks. "I'm mad to hear what it is."

Arthur explained at length.

"You see," he concluded, "we'll need your help in a lot of things. First, we'll want to make the map look like an old one—but we don't know how."

Robin Hood kept translating to Mr. Lafayette. Apparently he realized that the

THE CONSPIRACY CONTINUED 177

Big Eight would not stop to put their talk into French—they were too excited.

"I can help you there," Robin Hood declared. "I know just what you do to make a map look old."

"Then," Harold added, "we've got to make the boxes look old. That's a very hard proposition."

"You see," Arthur suggested, "there's some old boards in the wood-shed. They came out of the barn when it was made into a gym. But I don't know how an old box was put together."

"Either they dovetailed it," Robin Hood said, "or they dowelled it with wooden pegs. We'd have to have a regular carpenter to do that for us."

"Aren't there some old boxes in the attic?" Bunny demanded.

"Lots of them," Robin answered. "I have investigated the attic. But they aren't quite old enough."

"But how could we make them look old," Laura asked, "if we had them made now? I mean those pegs. They'd be all bright, new wood, wouldn't they?"

"Oh, there are plenty of ways of making

things look old," Robin Hood explained. "The process is called antiquing. I think we can fix the boxes up just as easily as the map. Besides, after they have been buried in the ground for two or three months, they'll look old enough. What's your next difficulty?"

Arthur answered. "When we cut the arrows in the rocks, how can we make them look old, too?"

"If we could scrape some lichens off a rock and glue them to the arrow," Rosie suggested brilliantly.

Everyone laughed.

"It's the hardest thing in the world to scrape lichens off from a rock," said Robin Hood. "However, weathering those arrows is the least of our troubles, I'll show you about that later."

"Then the last problem," Arthur concluded, "is how are we going to manage to make Mr. Westabrook and Billy see the arrow?"

This puzzled the ingenious and inventive Bunny. It even puzzled the fertile and resourceful Robin Hood.

"I thought and thought all the time we were dressing," Arthur began hesitantly, "and it seemed to me, that we might keep taking them to walk past the arrow until they saw it. But perhaps they never would notice it of their own accord. And if they didn't one of the girls might start to pick a flower."

"I'll plant a violet right in front of it," Rosie declared.

Again everyone laughed.

"And as she picked it," Arthur went on still intent on his plan, "she might say, 'Oh Mr. Westabrook, look! There's an arrow carved in this rock. What do you suppose it's there for?'"

For the third time the whole table laughed. The Big Eight, getting quite out of bounds, pounded applause on the table with their spoons.

"I think that's a wonderful idea," Bunny commented. "In fact I think your whole plan is wonderful."

"You see," Arthur said, continuing his story, "if Mr. Westabrook or Billy does say, 'I wonder what it means?' some one of us must ask, 'Do you think it has anything to do with Blanchemain the Pirate?' And then another one of us must say, 'Let's dig and see if there's anything there!' Then it's up to us. If Mr. Westabrook or Billy aren't interested, we can dig because *we* are. We'll find the first box with the map which might say something like this——"

Arthur's voice deepened, took on a sepulchral tone.

" 'Dig under arrow on pointed rock in front of middle one of three oaks between the big rock, shaped like a cow, and the small rock, shaped like a crescent.' "

"And is there on the place a big rock shaped like a cow and a small one shaped like a crescent?" Bunny inquired breathlessly.

"Oh, yes," Arthur answered. "Over by the cave are three oaks and a pointed rock in front. And there's a rock shaped like a cow lying down to the right and another shaped like a crescent to the left. I've noticed them a hundred times. Well, by this time," he went on, "perhaps Mr. Westabrook and Billy would be just as excited as we. Anyway I know I'd be as excited myself as though we were going to dig up a bucket of pieces-of-eight."

"So would I!" exclaimed the rest of the Big Eight.

"Well," Arthur concluded, "then we'll

dig—this time under the arrow on the pointed rock. And there we'll find another box. And in that other box will be—will be—will—well, *that's* the best part of the joke."

He went on to explain what the best part of the joke was.

"It's perfect!" Bunny applauded. "It's a story in itself."

CHAPTER XVII

THE RIFT

WORK on the Great Surprise began at once.

The next morning, the first thing after breakfast, children and grown-ups filed into the wood-shed to examine the old lumber which, at Mr. Westabrook's orders, had been left stacked up there. They poked about among the boards examining each one very carefully until they found some which bore a look of extreme age.

Rummaging about in the trio of old carpenters' chests which helped to furnish the wood-shed, they found bits of ancient ironwork, which had come out of the house from time to time—rusted hinges and locks.

"That's exactly what we need for the boxes!" Arthur exclaimed in an excited voice. "Let's look them over!"

They spread the bits of reddish metal on the floor and made their choice—two pairs of hinges, two old locks.

The next step was to get into communication with a carpenter. This Robin Hood accomplished for them over the telephone; made an appointment with a Mr. Eli Davis to come to the Little House as soon as possible.

Mr. Davis arrived in his little Ford that afternoon. When they explained what they wanted him to do, he became very interested although obviously he was puzzled at the order.

"I'll get them boxes to you in ten days," he promised, "and it will take a microscope to prove they weren't made a century ago."

He went away, packing the old boards, locks and hinges into his Ford.

Then came the equally important work on the map. When the Big Eight filed from the dining room into the living room that evening, they found that Arthur had covered the center table with old books—all open at maps.

"I thought you'd like to see what old maps look like," he explained.

The Big Eight circled the table like a flock of hovering birds.

"Oh, I love this one," Rosie exclaimed, "it's such a lovely color."

"This is my favorite!" Silva declared, "the lines are so beautiful!"

"I hope you'll have a ship sailing the ocean like this one," Maida exclaimed enthusiastically.

"And a lovely design like this one!" Laura added. "You see it tells where the points of the compass are."

"Now if that isn't like a gang of girls," Arthur commented, "to pick out maps because they have pretty colors, or drawings of ships, or points of the compass on them!"

"Well, what should we pick them out for?" Rosie demanded huffily.

"Oh, for correctness—and a lot of things," Arthur concluded a little vaguely.

"Well, I don't see what difference it makes," Laura backed up Rosie. "Ours is going to be a map of this coast and this country right round here. It isn't going to be exactly like any one of these maps. So I don't see why we can't decide the style we want."

"Yes," Maida carried on this contention, "so long as we're going to have a map, I don't see why it shouldn't be as beautiful as we can make."

THE RIFT

"If that isn't just like girls," Harold came to Arthur's rescue.

Dicky and Tyma said nothing—only listened.

"I guess," Arthur said with a slight lordliness of manner, "when it comes to this map business, you girls had better leave it to us boys. That's a thing girls wouldn't naturally know much about. It's the sort of thing boys can do much better."

The three grown-ups, Bunny, Mr. Lafayette, Robin Hood, were in the meantime standing about, listening to this conversation. They did not interrupt, although the faces of the two men immediately blanked and changing expressions flashed into Bunny's look. They waited.

"Well, I'm sure," Rosie said, "if you don't want me to help on your map, you're quite welcome to do it alone. It's going to be a lot of work."

"You don't hurt my feelings," Laura said, "by leaving me out."

"I should like to work on the map very much," Maida asserted angrily.

"So should I!" said Silva—but quietly.

"Well," Arthur decided, still with an air of authority, "this map-making is something that you girls can't do. So you will have to be content with helping to carry out the rest of the joke."

The girls did not answer. Rosie's brows, however, drew such a stormy line across her forehead that beneath, her eyes looked like thunder clouds. Maida's cheeks turned a pink that was almost purple; her lips set themselves together in a tight line; her azure eyes flashed. Laura's look grew icier as her scornful big blue eyes contemplated the boys, one after the other. Silva alone remained untouched by rage. Her soft face did not change, except that she cast her eyes down. In a little while the group broke up, distributed themselves in the direction of various duties.

"Bunny," Rosie asked, "may we girls come up to your room and talk with you for a little while?"

"I'd be delighted to have you," Bunny answered, exactly as though she had expected a question of this sort.

Once in Bunny's room, Rosie turned and closed the door.

"I want to tell you about this first, Bunny," she said, "because some one of the

THE RIFT

grown-ups ought to know it and I think you will understand as well as anybody could."

"Understand what?" Bunny asked pleasantly.

"We girls have been talking something over among ourselves," Maida took up the story, "getting sick of the way the boys are treating us."

"They expect us to do everything for them," Laura continued, "but they don't intend to do anything for us, and lately they've begun to leave us out of all their fun. Isn't that true, Silva?"

"Yes," Silva answered. "For instance, they're always going off on walks with Robin Hood. Their walks are not so long, but that we could go too. But they never invite us."

"And when we suggest going with them," Rosie broke in, "they always say this isn't anything that would interest girls, or it's too hard work for girls—oh, a lot of things. I'm sick of it!"

"What are you going to do about it?" Bunny asked quietly.

The girls looked at each other.

"You tell Bunny, Rosie," Maida directed, "you thought the plan up."

"We're going to pay them back," Rosie announced—announced calmly but with a light in her eyes that was half the fire of anger and half the flame of triumph.

"Pay them back," Bunny repeated. "Somehow I don't like that phrase—*pay them back*. How are you going to pay them back?"

"Well, perhaps we don't exactly mean that," Rosie said. "It's more that we want them to realize something. You see, Bunny, ever since we've been in the Little House, we've done part of the work here. Mr. Westabrook said he'd like us to help in the housekeeping, so that we'd always know how to run a house. We girls take care of our own rooms—sweep and dust and make the beds and wash the paint whenever it gets dirty—especially about the door knobs."

"But," Bunny questioned, "the boys take care of their rooms too, don't they?"

"Yes, but that's all. And there are a lot of other things that we girls attend to, partly because we want to help Granny and Mrs. Dore, and partly because we like to do them. But the boys don't know it——"

"Or if they ever did know it," Maida interposed, "they've forgotten about it."

"They just take it for granted," Laura said.

"Now what we girls intend," Rosie made further explanation, "is to stop helping in all little things. It doesn't mean that it will be any harder for Granny and Mrs. Dore. It will only mean that if the boys want those things done, they'll have to do them themselves. They won't like it either, believe me. You see, Bunny," she concluded triumphantly, "we girls are going on a strike."

CHAPTER XVIII

THE GIRLS WALK OUT

THE next morning after the usual cheerful exchange of morning greetings, the Big Eight seated themselves, unfolded their napkins and——

"Why—why— Where's my orange juice?" Harold demanded.

On the plate in front of him lay, round, golden and *unpeeled,* a big orange.

"And mine?" Dicky repeated.

"And mine?" Arthur added.

"And mine?" Tyma concluded.

Maida spoke, her voice a little shaky. "I usually squeeze the oranges for breakfast, but I didn't have time to do it for you boys this morning."

"Well, I notice you found time to do it for the girls," Harold remarked in an injured tone.

"Yes," Maida answered, her voice quite steady now, "I'll always have time to do it for the girls."

THE GIRLS WALK OUT 191

The boys attacked their oranges, first with knives, then with fingers. They made bungling work—Arthur particularly. He squeezed the orange juice first into Dicky's eyes and then into his own. Once he said, "I wish some nice girl would offer to do this for me!" But the girls remained silent, drinking their orange juice, and then turning to their breakfast food.

That afternoon, a rain came up and the Big Eight occupied themselves quietly in the living room. Suddenly Harold came storming down the stairs.

"Who put these handkerchiefs on my bureau?" he demanded in a heated tone. "Why, they haven't been ironed yet!"

"I did," Laura answered.

"What did you mean by that?" Harold turned on his sister.

"Oh, I haven't found time to iron them yet," Laura returned in an airy tone, "and I don't think I shall be able to do them this week at all, Harold. I'm afraid you boys will either have to learn to iron them yourselves or use them rough-dry."

"Use a handkerchief that's as rough as a —as a—as a sail cloth!" exclaimed the fastidious Harold. "I wouldn't think of doing such a thing. You've *got* to iron them, Laura."

"I certainly haven't *got* to do anything," Laura answered in a tone of which she, among all the members of the Big Eight, was the most perfect mistress—a maddeningly cool, slightly superior tone. "And I don't think I shall ever do any more ironing. Mr. Westabrook didn't ask me to do it, nor Granny nor Mrs. Dore. I just started it of my own accord. And now I find I'm too busy to keep it up."

Harold glared at his sister.

"I suppose," Arthur put in, "you've decided not to press our ties any more. I noticed they haven't been pressed this week."

"Yes," Laura replied, still maddeningly superior, "I think I'll give up trying to keep your ties pressed. There are *so* many other things that interest me more."

By this time, even Tyma and Dicky were glaring at Laura. She sustained that glare with a most candid look of innocence in her deep blue eyes.

That noon at dinner, "I'm sorry that there isn't going to be any pudding for you

THE GIRLS WALK OUT

younger ones," Mrs. Dore announced to the boys.

"No pudding, Mother?" Dicky quavered. "Oh, I know," he said brightening, "you mean we're going to have ice cream."

"No," his mother said, her big brown eyes innocent of guile, "there isn't any ice cream either. There is nothing to eat after the salad."

"Why, Mother!" In Dicky's voice, usually so amiable, there was a note of hostile surprise. "How does it happen that we're not going to have any pudding?"

"It's my fault," Rosie burst in swiftly. "I think you boys have probably forgotten. But you see ever since we've been in the Little House, I've made the puddings three times a week. But I've been so busy today that I couldn't find time. And I'm afraid after this, we'll have to go without dessert on those days. I don't see how I'm going to keep making puddings with all the other work I have to do."

"Seems to me you girls are getting pretty lazy all of a sudden," Tyma commented.

"I certainly am," Laura admitted.

That night when they came into the living room, Arthur went to his accustomed place at the living-room table.

"Where's my ink?" he demanded in an injured voice. "And my pencils? And where's the pile of books that I left on the table last night? Where are they all?" he went on in an alarmed tone. "Generally when I come here all my things are piled up."

"Yes, Arthur," Silva answered in her very sweet, very low voice, "I always collect them for you when I dust this room. You see Florabelle fixes the room up every day, and she's apt to put things anywhere. But before dinner I come down here and get out the games, and I always see that your books and working materials are piled at your end of the table."

"Then why aren't they there now?" Arthur asked in an aggressive voice.

"Well, you see," Silva went on in her little silver thread of a voice, "I've been so busy today that I didn't have time to do that. And I'm afraid I can't promise that I'll ever do it again—I'm so busy all the time."

Arthur's brow grew black. "I'd like to know what's the answer to all this funny

THE GIRLS WALK OUT 195

business," he said. "I didn't think of this until just this minute. But this is the fourth thing you girls generally do that you're too busy to do now. What's it all about anyway?"

"I'll tell you what it's about, Arthur Duncan," Rosie answered, her eyes shooting sparks. "We girls are on a strike."

"On strike!" Arthur repeated incredulously. "What do you mean by that?"

"Just exactly what I say," Rosie answered. "We girls have got tired of the way you boys are treating us. You've gradually pushed us out of everything. You go on long walks and excursions with Robin Hood and you never invite us to go with you, although we can walk just as far as you. You play all kinds of games in the Gym, and you never ask us to join you, although there are plenty of them that we could play. You made your ice-house and wouldn't let us help. We stood those things, but now there has come something we won't stand. And that is—not letting us work on the pirate's map for the joke we're playing on Mr. Westabrook and Billy. You think you're so awfully smart about maps, Arthur Duncan! And you *do* make nice maps.

But Silva's maps put it all over yours. They're much more beautiful. So that if any single one among us is to make that map, it ought to be Silva. But of course no *one* of us should make it. We all ought to help," Rosie paused, breathless.

"So," Laura went on swiftly with the tale, "we girls have decided that if you can't do anything for us, we can't do anything for you. If you want orange juice in the morning instead of oranges, and if you want your handkerchiefs ironed and your ties pressed, if you want any puddings, and if you want your things all tidied up in the living room—then you must be just as nice to us."

"Because," Maida took up the thread, "we don't *have* to take care of any of those things, and we don't like them enough to do them for four ungrateful boys."

"So," Silva concluded, "this is all we have to say. We've told you where *we* stand. Now everything is up to *you*."

With a very dignified air, the four girls arose and filed out of the room.

During all this, Bunny, Mr. Lafayette and Robin Hood had kept complete silence. Mr. Lafayette could not of course follow the argument, but he studied the excited faces of the two groups with a growing interest. Robin Hood's face remained as quiet as a mask. Bunny's alone showed something that was like a smile of triumph.

"I'm sure you boys will want to talk this over alone," she said rising and following in the wake of the departing strikers.

For a long time the boys—their voices extremely subdued—stayed in the living room talking with Mr. Lafayette and Robin Hood.

CHAPTER XIX

A WINTER PICNIC

THE next morning was clear and cold. It had snowed in the night and the world lay under a white coverlet. When the girls came down to breakfast, they found only Bunny awaiting them.

"The boys got up early and went off somewhere with Robin Hood," she answered their surprised inquiries.

"Oh," Rosie exclaimed with flashing eyes, "I just despise those boys! Think of their leaving again——"

"I think you'll find a message on your plates," Bunny said twinkling and dimpling. "It may reconcile you to their absence."

It was true. On each plate lay an envelope, the address scrawled in a boyish hand. Maida opened hers first; read it aloud. "'The boys of the Big Eight request the pleasure of your company at a winter picnic to be given at six o'clock tonight by the

A WINTER PICNIC

side of the Magic Mirror. The boys of the Big Eight will call for you at half-past five.' "

The other three invitations were duplicates of this.

The four girls looked at each other in amazement; looked at Bunny.

"Apparently," Bunny declared, "they've made up their mind to mend their ways."

"A winter picnic!" Rosie declared, "what do you suppose it will be like?"

"I haven't any idea," Maida answered.

"Let's ask Granny and Mrs. Dore what they're going to do," Laura suggested.

Even before drinking their orange juice, they pelted into the kitchen. Both the older women were extremely uncommunicative.

"Oh, but you know something, Granny Flynn," Maida charged, "I can tell by that wicked look in your eye."

Granny laughed and so did Mrs. Dore; but they kept their smiling lips closed.

"Are the boys coming back to lunch?" Rosie asked.

"I belave not," Granny answered.

Rosie groaned. "I shall die of curiosity between now and half-past five."

"Well there's only one thing to do,"

Maida suggested, "and that's to work so hard that the minutes will fly."

The girls took Maida's advice. After breakfast, they became extremely busy. But they complained that the minutes did not fly. In fact Silva suggested with one of her occasional flashes of drollery that they did not even walk—that they actually hobbled. Rosie added that they might have gone lame or tied weights on their feet. And Maida embroidered this theme, advancing the theory that the minutes were actually paralyzed and could only drag one foot after the other.

"Wouldn't it be awful," Laura suggested "if time should suddenly stop still like a clock that's run down, and half-past five would never *never,* come."

The girls moaned at this suggestion and turned more frantically to their work. They dusted their rooms with a minute care; arranged and re-arranged closets and bureau drawers. With a fine cloth they went over all the maps in the map room. They looked through the book-shelves in the library, re-united long-lost first, second, third, fourth and fifth volumes. They even appealed to Granny Flynn; and asked to be allowed to

A WINTER PICNIC 201

put in order both the china closet in the dining room and the pan closet in the kitchen.

Granny Flynn accepted all this assistance.

Finally half-past four came and five and quarter past. At half-past, the girls were sitting all bundled up with worsted caps which came down over their ears, sweaters under winter coats, mufflers and warm gloves. It was quite dark. Suddenly outside they heard a scraping sound and the bell rang. They rushed pell-mell to the door.

Lined up in front of the house, each standing in front of his sled, stood the four boys. As though they had been drilled to do this, their right hands all went to their hats, and as they lifted them they said in a chorus, "Permit us to drive you to the Magic Mirror."

Very much embarrassed, blushing and casting down their eyes, but giggling at intervals, the four girls took their places, one on each sled. The boys started off over the snow in the direction of the Magic Mirror. The trip took twenty minutes. It would not have taken so long if the boys hadn't started racing each other, and twice turned their fair passengers into a snow drift. However, no bones were broken and, in fact, the giggles were very noticeably increased by these accidents. In the meantime, it was growing darker and darker.

Suddenly, "I see the moon," Maida exclaimed. "How big and beautiful it looks rising over the snow."

Above the white line of the horizon was lifting an enormous disc of rose-colored, duskily-mottled gold.

"It looks," Silva said dreamily, "as though it were a disc for a giant's phonograph."

"I see a light, too," Rosie exclaimed.

In the direction of the Magic Mirror flared first one big blaze; then another.

The boys turned toward it.

"It's a bonfire!" Laura declared.

"It's two bonfires," Rosie corrected Laura.

"Oh, and there's Robin Hood," exclaimed Silva.

"And Mr. Lafayette," exclaimed Maida.

"And Bunny!" exclaimed Laura.

"Now how did she leave the house?" Rosie asked in a baffled voice, "without our seeing her?"

A WINTER PICNIC

It *was* two bonfires; and it *was* Robin Hood and Mr. Lafayette and Bunny. When the girls jumped off the sleds, they discovered that Robin Hood was very busy cooking their dinner. The boys began to set the table, which consisted of three smooth broad boards resting on a pair of trestles. The girls offered to assist. The boys rejected these offers with politeness but extreme firmness.

After a while the dinner was announced.

And such a dinner!

Thick juicy steak; big baked potatoes; steaming cocoa; bread, already buttered; baked apples with plenty of sugar and cream. Those who sat at the ends of the tables near the fires were always too hot, and those who sat in the middle were always too cold. However, they accepted these pleasant hardships with great grace and humor. As fast as the two pairs at the ends got "roasted brown"—the phrase was Rosie's—they exchanged with the pairs in the middle. However the hot cocoa did much to keep their temperatures even.

After supper the boys, still politely refusing the girls' assistance, burned up the paper plates and napkins; and still adamant so far as help was concerned, washed in melted snow the tin cups, the silver knives and forks. For a while the entire party stood about the fires, talking. Then suddenly, "How would you girls like a little skating?" Robin Hood asked.

"We'd love it," Maida said, "but we haven't our skates with us."

"Oh, the boys saw to that," Robin Hood answered.

In another moment a boy was kneeling in an attitude of great deference before each of the girls, was strapping on her skates. For an hour on the smooth, hard surface of the Magic Mirror the party played skating games—hockey and tag. They even danced together. At the end, Bunny and Robin Hood organized a Virginia Reel—perhaps the most original Virginia Reel in the history of the world. There was no time during its progress when at least one pair of dancers was not flat on the ice, waving skates in the air and laughing so hard that it was almost impossible to get up. And there was one moment in the last reel when they were all down.

When the dance was over, Robin Hood announced that it was time to go home.

A WINTER PICNIC

Again the boys invited the girls to take their places on the sleds. Bunny, Mr. Lafayette, Robin Hood walked back together.

"Oh, girls," Robin Hood exclaimed suddenly, as they stood warming themselves before the living-room fire, "the boys and I are going to take a long hike tomorrow. Would you like to come with us?"

"*Would we?*" Rosie answered.

"Oh, how lovely," Maida breathed.

"I've been perfectly—*wild* to go on one of those hikes," Laura declared innocently.

"*I can't wait!*" Silva whispered.

When the boys came to breakfast the next morning, there was a glass of orange juice at each place.

CHAPTER XX

HAPPY DAYS AND HOLIDAYS

MORE snow! More snow! And still more snow! Soon the children were living in a perpetual white world. The grown-ups encouraged them to stay out in it as long as they could. However, there came blizzard days when life had to be lived indoors. And in those days after the morning's work was over, the Big Eight usually made for the Gym. How much the children enjoyed their big new toy, it would be impossible to describe. Once, Billy Potter said, "I expected you boys to get a lot of fun out of this, but I must confess I was a little dubious about the girls."

"Well, of course one reason we're getting so much fun out of it," Rosie answered with a flash of Rosie's spirit, "is that we went on strike."

The boys always looked a little sheepish when the girls referred to their strike; always changed the subject as soon as possible. It was certainly true that the girls got a good deal of fun out of the Gym. The instant she entered the Gym, Rosie went straight to the traveling rings. She was always in the air. The other girls enjoyed this form of locomotion too, but they never became so expert as Rosie.

Laura, who to some degree shared her brother's physical cleverness, matched his accomplishments in athletics with accomplishments in dancing. Mr. Lafayette had started a class in fencing. Laura took to it just as Harold did; actually became more expert than any of the girls. She developed a lunge so swift and well-balanced as to bring "Ahs" of admiration from her teacher. The rest distributed their attentions impartially among the apparatus of the Gym, although perhaps no one enjoyed all forms of exercise as Silva and Tyma. Arthur, who had an ambition to become a strong man, devoted himself to the chest-weights.

All their other work was going on. The Big Eight could chatter quite creditable French now. Regularly every evening still, they gathered about the piano and sang French songs with Mr. Lafayette. Even in the face of temptation offered by the first snow, Arthur and Harold had managed to keep up their piano practice. They had not, as they hoped, accomplished their first duet by Christmas, but they achieved it on New Year's Day; played it that evening, to the tumultuous applause of the rest of the Big Eight.

All the others had given up painting. Silva alone continued steadily to work, with Robin Hood. It gradually came out that she wanted to finish a picture, of which she would not to be too much ashamed, to present to Mr. Westabrook when he returned. Robin Hood still put a problem on the blackboard every morning. Bunny still engineered their spelling matches.

"Remember we're going to school!" the children often said to each other. But they always laughed when they said it.

"Remember we're studying arithmetic!"

"Remember we're studying geography!"

"Remember we're studying history!"

"Remember we're writing compositions!"

Robin Hood continued to tell them enchanting adventures. And now he was interesting them in the books of famous discoverers and explorers.

"What I like about books," Rosie said once, "is that you can explore Africa when the snow is on the ground here. That's the time to explore Africa anyway. And the time to go to the North Pole or the South Pole—in books—is when it's so hot at home that you can scarcely breathe."

The Adventures of the Big Eight had grown to ten chapters. *The Little Tourists in the Southwest* had grown to nine. The children were very proud that they had beaten Bunny by one chapter. They were still trying to write chapters as long as possible. But although they embodied in each chapter the best ideas in the compositions of the entire Big Eight, they yet could not write so long a chapter as Bunny.

Yes, January and February were packed with out-door sports. Snow came and stayed; came again and stayed; continued to come and continued to stay. The world seemed to be a flying dazzle of lacy flakes, of glare ice, of long, sun-shot, snow-swept coasts.

Holidays appeared at intervals and in

some way the Big Eight celebrated them all. Lincoln's Birthday came, and they celebrated it quietly with an interesting talk from Robin Hood about Lincoln and the slaves and the Civil War.

St. Valentine's Day came. This brought of course a wild morning and a wilder evening; for everyone in the house had made valentines for everyone else. Many-colored envelopes shot from every direction onto the inhabitants of the Little House. They flew through windows and doorways; they appeared upon plates and on sofa cushions. At dinner they came in with every course.

"I'm almost afraid to turn on the hot water faucet," Rosie said once, "for fear nothing but valentines will flow out of it."

They found it difficult to think of anything original to do for Washington's Birthday. But they finally decided to have an hour of patriotic songs. By this time they had not only learned the French national hymn, but Mr. Lafayette was beginning to teach them the Italian national air. Indeed he sang songs of many countries, and the children could often join with him in the choruses. After the hour of singing, Robin Hood told them something about Washington's life; he gave them some idea of the causes of the Revolution, described the seven long years of military struggle. Every few minutes something he said sent them to the maps.

Arthur became fired with the idea that he would like to make a map illustrating the Revolution. Thrilled by this plan, he further declared that he would like to make maps illustrating all of America's wars— the Indian Wars; the Revolution; the War of 1812; the Mexican War; the Civil War; the Spanish War.

"You're biting off more than you can chew, young man," Robin Hood warned him. "We'll wait until you're a little older before we start anything so ambitious as that."

"Dear me!" Maida mourned once. "We're running out of holidays. There's nothing before Memorial Day, and that's the last of May."

She made that statement one day. The next——

When she came to lunch, there lay on her plate a letter with a foreign stamp.

"From Father!" Maida said, her face

sparkling with delight. "Granny, may I read this letter now? I do so want to know about my father's plans."

Granny gave her permission. Maida read, absorbed. Suddenly she burst into a ripple of laughter.

"I said we hadn't any more holidays to celebrate before the thirtieth of May," she said, "but listen to this. Father says, 'I shall land in Boston the last day of March. I shall be with you that night and all the next day.'"

The children applauded this good news. But Maida's mirth continued to ripple in peal after peal of laughter.

"Don't you see," Maida went on, her voice rising to a high note, "don't you see that he's going to be with us on April Fools' Day? That's the day of all days for him to find the two boxes."

"April Fools' Day!" Rosie said.

And, "April Fools' Day!" they all said.

Even the grown-ups laughed as they repeated, "April Fools' Day!"

CHAPTER XXI

THE PREPARATIONS

THE preparations that Arthur now called the Great April Fools' Joke went merrily on. Everything that could be done indoors however had been done.

Long ago Mr. Davis had delivered the boxes. About the same size, of the old constructed weather-beaten wood, in which the very dowels had been made to look ancient; with hinges and locks of a convincing rustiness—they might have come from some garret filled with antique treasure.

The map was finished too. And the children were constantly going to the drawer of the little table in which it reposed, to unfold it and gaze admiringly down upon their masterpiece. They oh'd and ah'd over it.

It was quite small—just long enough, when rolled, to lie tautly in one of the boxes. Robin Hood had cut from an old book the page of ancient paper, on which it was drawn. Robin Hood had soaked and re-soaked that paper in strong coffee; had even submitted it to certain corrosive acids until it had attained a look of great age. Then had come the period of map drawing. Here Robin Hood gave no help.

"The more it looks like *your* map," he explained, "the more it will look like a *pirate's* map. Pirates, generally speaking, were not educated people. Their maps would be very crude and simple."

This remark made such an impression on Arthur that one night, with a sigh of real regret, he said, "I'm just dying to do this map—I mean with Silva's help. But of course it ought not to be drawn by a person who's had as much practice in map-making as I. But by somebody who hasn't done much of it. Now which of us makes the worst maps?"

"Rosie!" the rest of the Big Eight shouted instantly.

"Thank you for the compliment," Rosie said with emphasis.

"Then you've got to draw the map, Rosie," Arthur decreed.

"But I don't want to draw the map," Rosie asserted with spirit. "Thank you most to death for asking me."

THE PREPARATIONS 217

map-box in it, covered it up and trampled it down into shape.

"We'll get some turf and put it down here," Robin Hood said. "I'll fix that!"

That afternoon they dug the second hole, and in it placed the second box with its mysterious contents. Then as before, they filled the cavity.

"Gee, I'm glad that's done!" Arthur exclaimed, as they started home. "I feel as though the joke was really going to work. Now tomorrow we'll have to start carving those arrows."

The next day brought weather even warmer. Immediately after breakfast, the Big Eight were on the trail again, armed this time with chisels, hammers, and all kinds of digging and scraping instruments from screw drivers to ice picks.

Their original plan included the carving of three arrows, pointing downward on the rock which marked the map-box. After consultation with Robin Hood they marked out the arrows; began to chip. They took turns, boys and girls.

"Oh, why did you say we'd have three arrows?" Harold groaned. "Why won't one arrow be enough?"

"It's got to be three arrows," Maida said with a sudden air of authority. "Things in stories always go by threes or sevens. Perhaps we ought to have seven arrows," she said wickedly.

A chorus of groans filled the air.

"All right, have three," Harold said in a resigned tone. And three there were.

The three arrows completed—and a fairly creditable performance they were—Arthur stood off and surveyed the job.

"How are we going to make those marks look old?" he said in a despairing voice. Falling on his knees before them he began frantically rubbing the clear gray of the fresh rock with mud.

"That won't do it, Arthur," Robin Hood interposed. "I've thought of that. I'm going to give those arrows a little medicine." He took from his pocket a leather case, and opening it displayed a file of tiny bottles. With a wad of cotton, which he produced from the same pocket, he began to rub the arrows with a fluid which he poured from one of the bottles.

"It looks as though you were giving them argyrol!" Rosie commented.

"It's a much more powerful thing than

argyrol, Mistress Rosie Brine," Robin Hood answered. "It's an acid and it has a bite like a mad dog. By tomorrow our spick and spandy arrows will begin to appear quite stained. I'm coming back occasionally to give them other treatments. By the time Mr. Westabrook arrives, they will look quite as though Blanchemain and his pirates had carved them."

Very faithfully Robin Hood carried out his plan. Whenever the weather was fine, he and the children set off in the direction of the Great April Fools' Joke, and on every visit Robin Hood treated the three arrows of the one rock and the one arrow of the other with one mixture or another from a little bottle. The children watched their carvings grow browner, as though each day age had, with its withering hand, pressed harder and harder upon them.

"I think," Bunny said one night, just as they were about to engage in a spelling match, "that we ought to begin to think about how we're going to call Mr. Westabrook's attention to the Rock of the Three Arrows. You see we must do it very casually—or he'll suspect something. Now the only way for us to make it natural is to plan just what everybody is to say, and when he's to say it. And then rehearse, so that it will go off just like a play."

Laura bounced in her chair. "Oh, why don't we give a play some time?" she asked breathlessly.

"We will," Bunny promised, "but not this spring. The Great April Fools' Joke is going to be this spring production. We'd better decide all these things now. We might begin the rehearsals—so that it will go off like clock-work."

Immediately everyone became animated. Everyone made suggestions.

Suddenly the telephone rang.

"Maida," Robin Hood, who answered it, said, "you're wanted on the telephone."

"A telegram for Miss Maida Westabrook," came the operator's voice in Maida's ear.

MISS MAIDA WESTABROOK
THE LITTLE HOUSE
SATUIT
MASSACHUSETTS

I AM LANDING IN NEW YORK STOP WILL COME WITH BILLY POTTER TO THE LITTLE HOUSE ON

MORNING OF MARCH THIRTY-
FIRST FOR VISIT OF TWO DAYS
STOP GREETINGS AND BEST
WISHES TO EVERYBODY STOP
DEAREST LOVE TO YOU MY LITTLE
DAUGHTER
        (Signed) Jerome Westabrook

CHAPTER XXII

MR. WESTABROOK ARRIVES

IT was the morning of the thirty-first.

"Oh, will that old clock ever get to eleven?" Maida moaned.

"It seems as though I'd been up all night," Rosie declared.

"If I had to live through another hour of this," Laura threatened wildly, "I should drown myself in the Magic Mirror."

Silva alone said nothing. She was reading *Little Women*.

The boys were wasting no time in talking. But they were wandering through the house, as Bunny said, "like a pack of hungry wolves seeking whom they could devour."

"Nothing *could* go wrong." Arthur paused once in front of Robin Hood.

"I can't see how," Robin Hood answered calmly. "I can't think of any situation that we haven't prepared for."

"A quarter to eleven," said Rosie, who

for an hour—at fifteen minute intervals—had been announcing the time.

"Only fifteen minutes more!" Dicky exclaimed. "Only fifteen minutes more!"

Five minutes passed and ten and—suddenly from the distance came the sound of a prolonged hoot. The children did not put their outside clothes on—they seemed to dive, head first, into them. They tore through the hall, out the front door and down the path. In the distance the big car was speeding—literally speeding—up the road. The children streaked, like the tail of a swiftly moving ground-kite, in that direction.

Presently the car stopped and they swarmed into it. When it arrived at the Little House, Maida was sitting on her father's lap, and the rest of children hanging on by hands and feet and eyelids. Mr. Westabrook freed himself and leaped out. He and Billy shook hands with the grown-ups. There came the confused exchange of greetings, questions and answers which always mark the reunion of friends. The children in the meantime stood about, first on one foot and then on the other—finally jumped up and down with impatience.

"Nobody knows how glad I am to be here!" Mr. Westabrook exclaimed. "This spring air tastes good, I can tell you."

"How are you feeling?" Robin Hood asked.

"A little tired," Mr. Westabrook answered. "I didn't sleep very well last night on the train."

"Not so tired that you can't take a walk with us, Father," Maida exclaimed anxiously.

"Oh, no, I'll take a walk with you—later though."

Mr. Westabrook went into the house, the children dancing round him in excited groups. He shook hands with Granny Flynn and Mrs. Dore; asked innumerable questions; answered as many more.

"Yes," Mr. Westabrook concluded, "I'm glad to be here. I'm tired. I want a rest."

"But you *can* take a walk with us?" Arthur asked.

"Oh, yes, I can take a walk," Mr. Westabrook said, "tomorrow after I get rested."

The children looked furtively at each other.

"We did want to take a walk this after-

MR. WESTABROOK ARRIVES 225

noon," Rosie said. She added a little lamely, "The violets might be out and the anemones——"

"Well, we'll see after dinner," Mr. Westabrook declared.

It was not so very long before the dinner bell rang. All during the meal Mr. Westabrook talked about his travels. Bunny, Billy, Mr. Lafayette, Robin Hood were naturally very much interested; in their turn they asked question after question. But the Big Eight did not prolong the conversation by a single inquiry. Nervously they wriggled in their chairs, nervously they scuffed the floor; nervously they kicked their feet against the table-legs.

"How soon do you think you'd feel like taking a walk, Mr. Westabrook?" Harold inquired with a polite eagerness, as they got up from the table.

"Oh, just as soon as I've had my cigar," Mr. Westabrook answered comfortably.

The grown-ups still continued their carefully casual talk. The children sat on the edges of their chairs and watched, as though fascinated, the tip of Mr. Westabrook's cigar. A collar of white ash appeared on it;

grew in length, fell from it; another and another. Presently he rubbed the stub out in an ash tray.

"Now will you go to walk, Mr. Westabrook?" Laura cried.

"Just one more smoke," Mr. Westabrook pleaded.

He lighted another cigar. For a minute the Big Eight, discouraged, settled back in their seats. But at the end of another minute they were all again sitting upright on the edges of their chairs, their eyes riveted to the red tip of Mr. Westabrook's cigar.

A collar of ash appeared; developed, dropped into the tray . . . another . . . another . . . and another . . . Mr. Westabrook rubbed out the burned end of the stub.

The children jumped to their feet. Silva, Tyma and Dicky spoke together.

"Now will you go to walk with us, Mr. Westabrook?" they pleaded.

"I never saw children so crazy to walk before," Mr. Westabrook commented good-naturedly. "Yes, I'll enjoy some fresh air." He added, "You'll have to guide the expedition though, you children. I haven't walked in the woods round the Little House for—I don't know how many years."

Guide the expedition! Rosie suddenly disappeared into the hall. Afterwards they learned she'd gone there to laugh. But in another moment, sober-faced, she was back among them again. Silent now, they all got into their hats and coats. They poured out of doors.

"Why, Mr. Westabrook, at last you're really going to walk with us," Dicky commented in a feeble voice.

"Yes," Mr. Westabrook answered gravely, "and you're not a bit more happy over it than I am."

CHAPTER XXIII

THE WALK

CURIOUSLY enough, so far as the Big Eight were concerned, the first part of the walk was made in complete silence. Every one of them was thinking of his own part in the coming drama. Every one of them showed that within him a sense of responsibility struggled with a sense of anxiety. Arthur Duncan was actually pale. However, quite resolutely he put himself in the lead. Trailing him, came the rest of the Big Eight. Behind them, came the five grown-ups all talking busily.

The ground was comparatively dry, for there had been a week of spring sunshine. Green of grass showed everywhere. Trees and shrubs were uncovering points of emerald fire. At first Mr. Westabrook did not seem to notice where they were going.

On they went.

"I have seen the spring in Sicily," Mr. Westabrook said, "in Northern Italy, in

THE WALK

Paris, in London. Four springs, all in one year. And now I'm getting a fifth—the one I love most in the world—the New England spring."

On and on they went.

They were approaching the Rock of the Three Arrows. The children tried not to look at it; fixed their eyes on points as far away as possible. Occasionally, however, their glances lighted on it.

The play was ready to begin.

Quite casually, Rosie detached herself from the group. With a clear, "I wonder if the mayflowers have begun to sprout," she began studying the ground by the side of the path. Slowly and indirectly, she approached the rock. Suddenly she knelt down close to it.

"Oh, see what funny marks there are on this rock," she opened the play in a loud clear voice.

The rest of the Big Eight flocked about her.

"Why they're arrows!" Arthur exclaimed, carrying on the dialogue.

"Let me see!"
"Let me see!"
"Let me see!"

The other children jostled each other a little, trying to examine the mysterious mark.

By this time the grown-ups had approached.

"What is it, children?" Mr. Westabrook asked mildly.

Now Maida entered the game. "There are such strange marks on this rock, Father!" Her eyes wandered to her father's face, back to the rock; stayed there.

Mr. Westabrook approached. "Why they look like arrows!" he exclaimed. "They are arrows," he decided. "Wouldn't you say they were arrows, Billy?" he asked.

Billy Potter came forward. He too examined the mysterious symbols. "They certainly are arrows," he agreed, "pointing very definitely downwards."

"How about it, Mr. Hood?" Mr. Westabrook called.

Thereupon Robin Hood came forward.

"Oh yes, those are arrows," he declared; "no mistake about that."

"Well—that's funny," Mr. Westabrook meditated. "I wonder what— Now who could have cut that there?"

This was Arthur's cue.

"You don't suppose, Mr. Westabrook," he said in a quavering voice, "that Blanchemain the Pirate could have done it?"

"Of course not!" Mr. Westabrook scoffed. "Most of the legends of Blanchemain the Pirate are just talk!" He stood for a moment silent, his eyes still fixed on the arrows.

"Of course they haven't anything to do with Blanchemain the Pirate," he declared a second time. "But it may point to something that's—" Again he fell into a sort of meditation. But his eyes remained fixed on the arrows.

The children stood breathless.

CHAPTER XXIV

MR. WESTABROOK DIGS

"ARTHUR," Mr. Westabrook spoke with a sudden sharp note of command, "you run back to the house and bring back two or three shovels and a pick-axe. Get Zeke to help you. I'm going to dig here. I want to see what those arrows are pointing at."

Arthur was off like a shot. The children, unable to contain themselves, scattered as though examining the nearby landscape for further rock-arrows. In as brief a time as possible, Arthur was back, his arms full of shovels—panting; Zeke beside him, his arms also full of shovels—and also panting. Mr. Westabrook seized one of the shovels.

"I'll dig first," he offered, "you others can spell me when I get tired."

He started vigorously to turn the earth over. Presently he took off his big overcoat and hung it on a tree-limb. He was working hard and the perspiration stood in great drops on his brow. After a while he said, "I'm too soft for any more of this. Here, Billy, you try for a while."

"I've been wild to dig ever since you found that arrow," Billy Potter declared. He attacked the earth with an athletic vim. He, too, perspired. He, too, took off his coat. He, too, kept doggedly at the job. Presently however, he relinquished the shovel to Robin Hood; mopped his face and put his coat on again. Mr. Westabrook and Billy stood in visible impatience while their successor worked.

The shovel went round the circle of men —and then the boys offered their help. They had been working for about an hour when Mr. Westabrook, who happened to be shoveling, suddenly exclaimed, "There! There! I've struck something!" Although he had been digging for a long time, he seemed to acquire new life. Billy took up another shovel and they worked together. The earth flew.

"It's a box!" Mr. Westabrook said in an excited tone.

"Wood!" Billy added in a tone no less excited.

Another moment—and the top of the box appeared. A few more moments and it was free from the earth. Mr. Westabrook lifted it out; began to fumble at the lock. Suddenly it broke in his hand. He lifted the cover.

This was Tyma's clue.

"Oh, let me see!" he called, crowding close. And then the Big Eight, one after another, took it up. The air rang with, "Let me see!" "Let me see!"

"It's nothing but a roll of paper," Mr. Westabrook exclaimed. His tone was casual but his air was excited.

He put the box on the ground, took out the roll. Even in that flash of observation, the Big Eight noticed how a month in the wet earth had added age to the look of both.

"It's a *map!*" Mr. Westabrook said. "Of all things—a map!"

His hands shook a little as he examined it. All the grown-ups had gathered about him; were studying the faded, ancient parchment.

And now came Dicky's cue.

"Oh, let me see!" Again the air rang with the children's cries of, "Oh, let me see!"

MR. WESTABROOK DIGS 235

Mr. Westabrook held the map low, so they could all look at it. And the Big Eight studied it with a very convincing air of seeing it for the first time.

"What do you suppose it means?" Mr. Westabrook was in the meantime asking the others.

"It certainly looks like Blanchemain the Pirate to *me*," Bunny declared, sparkling and dimpling.

"Well, the thing to do is to find out where the spot on this map is. I'd like to get a chance to read this writing," Mr. Westabrook said a little querulously.

The children moved away to give him light. Mr. Westabrook put on his glasses, " 'The three trees between the two rocks, one shaped like a cow, one shaped like a half moon. Under arrow on rock in front of middle tree.' "

"I must say that sounds like regular pirate stuff," he admitted. "But where is this spot?"

Harold swung in.

"Well, why don't we scatter through the woods," he suggested practically, "and see if we can find it?"

This was not Silva's cue. But in her soft

voice, she said, "Why don't we take the shovels with us—in case we have to dig?"

"Good idea!" Mr. Westabrook approved. "Zeke, you pick up the tools."

They scattered.

According to plan, Arthur struck out ahead in the right direction. The others sheered off in various directions. The sound of hurried footsteps, of voices calling to each other, filled the air on all sides. Suddenly Arthur's voice rang out in a loud whistle. He came tearing back.

"I've found it!" he exclaimed triumphantly, "I've found it!"

From all directions the group raced to his side; streamed after him as he ran.

"There!" he said suddenly, "Isn't that a cow-shaped rock? And isn't that a half-moon shaped rock? And isn't that the pointed rock in front of the middle tree?"

"It must be," Mr. Westabrook agreed in a voice that had become almost hysterical, "for there's an arrow on it. Let's dig as we have never dug in our lives!"

He himself took the spade from Zeke's shaking hands. But although he attacked the job with great zest, it was apparent that he was getting tired.

MR. WESTABROOK DIGS 237

"You'll have to take it, Billy," he admitted after a few moments.

"You can't give it to me too soon," Billy commented. "I never was so excited in my life."

Robin Hood spelled Billy and Mr. Lafayette spelled Robin Hood. Again the boys took turns.

It was Arthur this time who exclaimed, "I've struck something!" And it was Mr. Westabrook who this time followed with "Wood!" He added, "It sounds just like the other!" And as before, he tore frantically with his shovel at the earth which surrounded the box.

"No wonder!" Billy said, "that it sounds like the other. It's a box exactly like it. I know this contains treasure! What do you suppose it is!"

Nobody answered. The Big Eight were exactly as excited as though they had no idea what it did contain. Billy reached down—his hands trembling too—and tugged the box out of the earth. He handed it over to Mr. Westabrook.

The children crowded about Mr. Westabrook. He wasted no time fiddling with this lock—he broke it open, lifted the cover.

Inside, wrapped in old, time-faded moth-eaten linen, lay what looked like two ancient packages. Mr. Westabrook picked up the first, unrolled it. There appeared in his hand a slim book—a very, very slim book—brilliantly bound in scarlet morocco, engraved with gold letters.

His eyes almost popping out of his head, he read the inscription. Then he burst into a roar of laughter. Hastily he unrolled the other. Appeared another slim scarlet, gold-inscribed book. Still roaring, he handed this to Billy. Mr. Westabrook read aloud:

THE ADVENTURES OF THE BIG EIGHT
by

Rosie Brine	Arthur Duncan
Silva Burle	Harold Lathrop
Tyma Burle	Laura Lathrop
Richard Dore	Maida Westabrook

Presented to Jerome Westabrook by the Authors.

In the meantime, Billy had been reading the inscription on the other book. He, too, was shaking with convulsions of laughter.

THE ADVENTURES OF THE BIG EIGHT
by

Rosie Brine
Silva Burle
Tyma Burle
Richard Dore

Arthur Duncan
Harold Lathrop
Laura Lathrop
Maida Westabrook

Presented to William Potter by the Authors.

"That's the best joke I've ever heard of in my life," Mr. Westabrook approved.

"Father," Maida asked, "do you know what day this is?"

Mr. Westabrook stopped short. "You little pirates—come to my arms!" he answered, "and let me hug every one of you! Of course! It's April Fools' Day."

XXV

GIFTS FOR EVERYBODY

DINNER was over before the hubbub in the Little House died down. Every time Mr. Westabrook caught Billy's eye, he burst into roars of laughter, and every time Billy caught Bunny's eye, *he* burst into roars of laughter.

Mr. Westabrook fired questions at the Big Eight until he had the whole story of the Great April Fools' Joke from the moment it dawned on the children that Maida's Little School was a myth, to the moment when they buried the two boxes in the earth. He was particularly entertained by the artful scheme by which he was led to the Rock of the Three Arrows. He even made the children rehearse the lines which led to his sending Arthur back for a shovel.

"Wait till I tell that story in Wall Street!" he said again and again. "I expect I'll lose any reputation that I have for knowledge of human nature."

After dinner was over and they were seated about the big fire in the living room, the talk turned to Maida's Little School.

"Shall I build you a real school, children?" Mr. Westabrook asked.

"No!" the Big Eight shouted in chorus.

"Do you want to keep on studying just the way you are at present?"

"Yes!" the Big Eight shouted.

"All right," Mr. Westabrook agreed, "that will save me a wad of money."

Presently Mr. Westabrook sent for the huge trunk which had come down to the Little House with him. Brought into the middle of the living-room floor and opened, it proved to be filled with packages. These were gifts for every member of the household of the Little House. For the girls were pieces of a lovely peasant china, desk-sets and porringers from Quimper. Immediately they found Quimper on the map of France. For the boys were bits of an interesting carved wood, desk-sets too and paper knives, from the Tyrol. Immediately they found the Tyrol on the map of Austria. For Granny and Mrs. Dore came beautiful warm shawls and gloves; thick and durable for the winter. delicate and pretty for the summer. For Bunny came a white Spanish shawl with long silk fringes, embroidered all over in flowers of strangely conflicting but strangely beautiful colors. For the three men came books.

This of course created another hectic interval. Everyone was screaming to everyone to look at his gifts. Presently the floor was strewn with paper and string and excelsior; dislocated boxes and wads of cotton wool.

"Oh," Rosie said once, "I don't think that little girl who lived through a year of Christmases had anything on us. It's Christmas all the time in the Little House!"

But after a while even this clamor died down.

"Let's clean up!" suggested Harold—always the neat one of the combination. "We can burn everything up in the fire and in ten minutes we'll look as good as new."

At once the Big Eight fell on the havoc they had created. Four of them picked up; two of them fed the flames; the remaining two wielded carpet sweepers.

"It's just as though a fairy waved a wand," Maida commented when the work

GIFTS FOR EVERYBODY 243

was done. "Presto!—and we're quite clean again."

"One of my pupils has something to show you, Mr. Westabrook," Robin Hood said, after they had re-seated themselves about the fire.

Silva blushed and dropped her shy eyes. "I'll have to go upstairs first."

She came back presently, carrying a small canvas.

"You see, Mr. Westabrook," she explained, "I've been taking painting lessons with Robin Hood. I told him that as soon as I could do anything good enough, I wanted to make a picture for you. I think this isn't very good myself, but Robin Hood seemed to think it would do."

She handed Mr. Westabrook the canvas.

Mr. Westabrook surveyed it carefully. Suddenly his eyes—keen to the verge of fierceness—dimmed a little.

"Thank you very much, Silva," he said. "You've got something in this that makes me think of my childhood."

The rest of the Big Eight crowded about him. It was a picture of the Little House with the snow on it.

"It has a quality," Billy Potter remarked.

"Yes," Robin Hood agreed briefly. "It's crude and lacking in firmness of course. Little technique yet, but there's something there."

"Now," Mr. Lafayette broke the spell with his swift staccato French, "*my* pupils have something to present to you too, Mr. Westabrook."

A little bashful, Harold and Dicky took their places at the piano and played through a duet—a duet new even to the Little House.

Mr. Westabrook listened attentively. At the end he joined in the swift applause of the Big Eight.

"I'm very proud of you!" he declared.

Harold and Dicky glowed with crimson delight.

"Well, now," Mr. Westabrook asked when the fourth excitement of April Fools' Day had died down, "what are we going to do this summer?"

The children stared at him in a panic.

"This summer?"

"Aren't we going to stay——"

"Must we leave——"

"We're not—" came a confused babble.

"Oh, I didn't mean that you were going away," Mr. Westabrook explained, "except perhaps all together, on a vacation somewhere. It was *that* I wanted to talk about. What would you like to do for a vacation?"

For a moment nobody spoke.

Then, "I know what they'd like to do, Father," Maida exclaimed, her eyes lambent with anticipation. "I'm sure I know: they'd like to camp out on Spectacles Island."

"Spectacles Island! Camp out on Spectacles Island!" Mr. Westabrook repeated. "Why, I haven't been on Spectacles Island since I was a boy. But if you want to do that, there's no reason why you shouldn't. So that's settled."

What endless fun and thrilling adventures the Big Eight have on Spectacles Island are told in *Maida's Little Camp*.

THE END

Maida's Little Shop
Primrose Court
Massachusetts
House Rock

Road to Maida's Little Camp in the Adirondacks

The Magic Mines
Fairy Ring
Tree House
★ The Little House

The Big House

The Stonecrop
Tilestone Hollow

Boy's House
Mess Hall
Girl's House

Tilestone Lane

Old Mill
MILL ROAD
Post Office
Brick House
The Barn